Acclaim for the Work of ELISSA WALD!

"A fine, passionately wrought novel from a writer whose prose I've long admired. Wald's vision of the world has much to teach us about the brevity of desire and the longevity of pain."
  —*Junot Diaz*

"Psychologically complex...Wald clearly knows her varied characters, whom she portrays in a sympathetic and unsparing light."
  —*Publishers Weekly*

"Remarkable and fascinating...Wald writes with a simplicity and frankness that are unusual but perfectly suited to her subject."
  —*Kirkus Reviews*

"Elissa Wald's style is both delicate and tough, her images haunting...I read it in one sitting, and I hope Wald receives the attention that she deserves for producing such a lovely and challenging work."
  —*Pat Califia*

"Elissa Wald is a brave, disturbing new voice in American fiction. She works all the margins of the wild side and brings us news from those frontiers that very few writers have dared approach."
  —*Pat Conroy*

I had time to take in every detail of the room—the black-and-white photo of the New York City skyline above the headboard, the heavy mauve curtains and the sheer white scrim behind them, the sparkling view through the window, the wide expanse of the bed.

I had time to take in every detail of him. He was handsome. His tie was loosened. His shoes were shined.

By the time he put his papers aside, my scant black panties were soaked through and there was an ache between my legs.

Finally he stood and slowly approached me until we were eye to eye. He had a few inches on me but not many. Looking straight into my gaze, he took off his belt and held it across my mouth.

"Kiss it," he said.

I kissed it.

"Kiss it like you'd like to kiss me," he said. "Kiss it like you love it."

My mouth opened and I tongued the leather, nipped at it like a kitten.

He took it away and cracked it against the wall next to my head. I whimpered in real fear. Then he wrapped it around my neck, sliding the leather end through the buckle so that it was at once a collar and a leash.

"Down on all fours," he said...

The
SECRET LIVES
of MARRIED
WOMEN

by **Elissa Wald**

A HARD CASE **CRIME NOVEL**

A HARD CASE CRIME BOOK
(HCC-113)
First Hard Case Crime edition: October 2013

Published by
Titan Books
A division of Titan Publishing Group Ltd
144 Southwark Street
London SE1 0UP

in collaboration with Winterfall LLC

Print edition ISBN 978-1-78116-262-0
E-book ISBN 978-1-78116-263-7

Design direction by Max Phillips
www.maxphillips.net

Typeset by Swordsmith Productions

The name "Hard Case Crime" and the Hard Case Crime logo
are trademarks of Winterfall LLC. Hard Case Crime books
are selected and edited by Charles Ardai.

Printed in the United States of America

Visit us on the web at www.HardCaseCrime.com

For Nikolai

and David

THE SECRET LIVES OF MARRIED WOMEN

PART ONE

The Man Under the House

1

Before that summer, *the summer of fear*—

It makes me cringe to know that I sound like a tabloid wife. I can't talk about what happened, even to myself, in a way that seems real. The words that come to me sound like something I've read in line at the supermarket.

Before the *summer of the stalker*, the summer *I looked at my husband and saw a stranger*, I was drinking in a bar with Rae and having a conversation about intimacy. It was a conversation I'd had many times before, with any number of thirty-something women who were worried about their chances of marrying in time to have children. Rae was thirty-six, the same age as me. She was our realtor, and it seemed she was also becoming a friend.

I had married just two years before, and now had a one-year-old daughter. (I was also a few weeks into my second pregnancy, but didn't know it yet.) As a result, my part in this time-worn dialogue had shifted from sharing the despair to dispensing counsel. Usually these women had spent their time—as I had, myself, until very recently—investing in a series of untenable characters, men whose inability to commit was as clear as the color of their eyes.

"I do want a family. I do," Rae was telling me. "And I know I've got to get on it soon. But I don't know if it would be fair to date right now because the truth is I'm still getting over someone else."

"Oh," I said. "So—you just ended a relationship?"

"If you can call it that."

"Let me guess: married man?"

"Worse than that. Even worse."

Hearing this, I couldn't help leaning in.

"Okay, how should I put this…let's call it a ten-year tryst. With a stone-cold thug. The guy's a gang leader and a dealer, he's done all kinds of time. And no, we didn't have an official relationship. We had nothing but insane, unbelievable sex. Trouble is, it was so good with him that no one else does it for me." Rae shot me a sidelong glance. "This is probably more than you wanted to know."

"Not to worry," I told her. "I want to know everything." This, at least, was the truth. And then I said my usual lines.

I know just what you're doing, because I spent almost two decades doing pretty much the same thing. If a man was married, or engaged, or living on another continent, or certifiably insane, or gay, or a priest, or a prison inmate serving a life sentence, I was all over him. A few of these categories were invented for emphasis, but not many. *On the other hand, if a man was single, appropriate, and well-intentioned, I couldn't run away fast enough. And when my relationships never seemed to work out, I decided I wasn't lucky in love. It took me years to understand that I was afraid of commitment myself, that the suffering was essentially self-inflicted. But even once I could see what I was doing, it took many more years to be able to change. Because that's what I was used to; that's where I was comfortable. It may have been bleak and lonely, but in some sense it was safe.*

And Rae asked the usual question in response. "So how did you cross the road?" she wanted to know. "How did you get to the other side?" And here I had another practiced answer.

You know, I don't think it's quite like that…at least for me, it's more of an ongoing process, and to be honest, I still struggle with it. But I think you have to reach the point where you want it more than you don't want it. Where you're ready—really ready—to let it into your life. I've come to believe that intimacy is available to anyone who's truly ready to give and receive it.

That conversation took place in the early spring.

2

A couple of months later, I was standing in front of our new home: a weathered split-level with cedar siding and asphalt roof shingles, set back from a somewhat busy street. This was in Vancouver, in Washington State, just a few miles north of Portland, Oregon. We would be moving in the next day.

I was at the edge of the driveway, scanning the street, when a man hailed me from the house under construction next door. A workman, well over six feet tall and broad-shouldered, with reddish-blond hair, a goatee, dusty clothes and work boots.

"Hey, are you moving in here? It's a great house. I'm Jack," he said, extending his hand. "I'm Walt's cousin." Walt was our house's former owner.

I was waiting for a house painter who was late. The night before, my husband had given him painstaking directions over the phone. Afterward he said the man sounded slow, or maybe drunk. I wasn't confident that he would show up.

"Do you know any painters?" I asked after shaking his hand.

"I'm a painter," he said. "What do you need painted?"

"Just one small room," I told him. "But it has to be today. I'd like it to air out overnight so my little girl won't be breathing in any paint fumes."

"Okay," Jack said. "Tell you what. Why don't I do it on my lunch break?"

"It'll take longer than a lunch break."

"Well, I can finish it tonight if need be."

"Really? Don't you want to see the room first?"

No need, he told me. He knew the room. (The little one

across from the master bedroom, yes? Yes.) He knew the house, he said, like it was his own. He'd do it for a hundred bucks.

This was an appealing offer, as the first painter had wanted one fifty. Just as I began to hope our original man wouldn't show up, his battered blue van pulled to the curb across the street.

"Just get rid of him," Jack urged. "Tell him you changed your mind."

"Well," I said. "I wish I could."

"Why can't you? Come on. I'll do it cheaper and better."

"I wouldn't feel right about it. He came all the way out here. But look," I said. I realized that for some reason I was anxious to appease him. "There's a lot more work we want done on this house. Our daughter's room was just the first thing. We want to strip the wallpaper in another room and paint that one too, and rip up some carpet and put down wood floors…"

When I brought the painter into the house, Jack came along so he could see what I wanted done. I showed him the alcove on the western side of the house, which was covered with garish electric-blue wallpaper. I thought that with a few adjustments, it would be ideal as a nursery for the baby due in November.

"Ah," he said. "The gun room."

"What?"

"This is the gun room. It's where Walt kept his rifles."

"Oh," I said. "Well, we'd like to make it a nursery now."

He had named his hundred-dollar price for the paint job on the spot, so now I tried to get an idea of how much he'd want to do other things. But here he became evasive, saying he charged by the hour and it was impossible to know how long such jobs would take.

"Like you never know what you're going to find under that wallpaper," he told me.

I went over to the wall and ripped off a long strip. "Well, here. Take a look," I said. I added that I didn't like to pay by the hour. "In general," I said, "jobs seem to take a whole lot longer when there's an hourly rate instead of a flat fee."

"Oh, hey, I don't screw around," he protested. "I get it done."

I didn't point out that at this very moment he was presumably on the clock of the owner next door while chatting me up.

"At the least," I said, "I'd need to know that a job wouldn't exceed a certain amount."

He looked at me as if I were speaking a foreign language, and I realized we were already on somewhat adversarial terms. I began to feel sorry I'd started talking with him at all.

"Well, look, I'm sure we'll figure something out," I said.

Instead of responding to this, he tilted his head and squinted at me. "You know," he said finally. "I think I've seen you some-place before."

"Maybe," I said. "We were in Portland for a year before buying this house, so if you get down there much…" But I didn't be-lieve he'd really seen me before; I didn't even think that *he* believed it. It was just something men said to get information.

It was true that we'd spent the last year renting a house in Portland. But when we were ready to buy, we were drawn to Vancouver, just across the Columbia River and the Washington state line. Here we were amazed by what we could afford: the lush green lawn and two-car garage, the split-level layout and vast kitchen. We loved the great room's vaulted ceiling and rough-hewn wooden beams, the floor-to-ceiling fireplace con-structed of river rock. For all this, we were willing to overlook the neighborhood's lack of charm, its absence of continuous sidewalks, and the fact that the area seemed to be all strip malls and chain stores.

It would be an adjustment, Stas and I kept saying to each other. Like the many other adjustments we'd made in such swift and recent succession. Stas had moved in with me after our second date and we'd married within the year. I was pregnant six weeks later, and we left New York City for the west coast a few months into the pregnancy. It was hard to leave Manhattan but even harder to imagine having children there: too expensive, too crowded, an endless hassle. If we stayed put, we told each other time and again, our kids would never get to play in the yard. In Manhattan, there were no yards.

Portland was full of yards, and there seemed to be two cats and a rosebush in every one of them. We rattled off the city's virtues to our friends back east: kind and gentle, laid back and easy, progressive and affordable and child-friendly. Portland offered easy access to the ocean, the mountains, the national forests and the desert. It was full of independent bookstores and galleries and museums.

Beneath all this was something harder to articulate: a certain ramshackle charm, an enchanted quality about even the modest houses and streets. Many of the homes brought the word *cottages* to mind, with their shingled sides and pitched roofs and smoking chimneys. Wildflowers were a fixture in almost every yard, and porches were often elaborately furnished, with porch swings and baby swings, rugs and chairs and end tables, prayer flags or paper lanterns. Little artisanal touches were everywhere: rectangles or diamonds of colored glass set into a wooden fence, roses trained painstakingly over a trellis, a mosaic of ceramic and china shards embedded in the cement of someone's front steps. Alleys crisscrossed the serene neighborhoods, and they could be mistaken for little country lanes with their hawthorn and honeysuckle and dirt paths worn smooth.

The only drawback was that so many others were in sudden

agreement about Portland's allure. Even as the real estate market was taking a hit across the nation, the housing prices there were skyrocketing. The other outposts of the city made Vancouver seem appealing. So here we were, first-time buyers with a home of our own. And I was having a room painted, because I could.

When I returned to the house later that afternoon to pay for the job, Jack appeared in the driveway again.

"Listen, I'll come up with a fair price to give you guys," he said. "I thought about what you were saying, and I get where you're coming from."

I told him I appreciated this. "There were just so many expenses involved in buying the house. More than we realized. So we want to rein in the spending for a while."

"Yeah, no, I get it," he repeated. "And like I said, I'll work out something you can live with."

I recounted this exchange to Stas when he came home from work. "So, you know, already it's awkward," I said. "I all but offered him this work, but he wouldn't say how much he'd want for it."

We were in the stripped living room of our Portland rental, sitting on boxes and eating takeout burritos on paper plates. Clara's crib had been dismantled and she was asleep in the Pack 'n Play.

"Why did you even start talking to him?" my husband asked, irritated. "Why didn't you wait to see if the painter would show up? You are too impatient."

"He started talking to me," I said.

"You should learn not to be so friendly."

"What the hell is that supposed to mean?"

Stas gave me a hard look and said nothing further.

I shouldn't have married him, I thought for perhaps the hundredth time.

❊

"Don't feel bad," Rae said a little later that evening, upon hearing the same story. She had come to drop off some house keys that Walt forgot to give us: one for the side door, another for the garage. "Your back was against the wall by then. You had one day to get the job done!"

I was happy to see Rae. Her loud pronouncements always gave me a lift.

"It's not like you would've had time for a comparison shop if the first guy never showed," she added.

"Well, exactly," I said.

"Just make him name his price before he starts. You're smart to want a flat fee. And listen, once you're settled in, we need to grab a drink. Maybe the middle of next week?"

The following morning, an unseasonably hot morning in May, we arrived at the house with our U-Haul in tow. My twin sister Lillian and her husband Darren were already parked out front; they had flown in from New York to help us move, and from here they would drive up to Canada to see Darren's father. "Look at that. Darren's rental," Stas said. "Is that a Mercedes…?"

This was something I never would have noticed. I could be close with someone for years and never notice what they drove, beyond a vague sense of its shape and possibly its color. Whereas Stas kept a vehicular inventory of his every casual acquaintance: the brand, the make, the year, how many miles it would get to the gallon.

Lillian emerged from the car: a lean and angular woman in faded blue jeans and a t-shirt, her dark hair swept back and held by a simple clip. She wore tortoiseshell glasses and no makeup: a slimmer, sensible version of me.

"It's lovely, Leda!" she said. "Look at your new yard. What a beautiful tree, and how great that there's a swing."

"Thanks so much for coming." We hugged hard and I breathed in her scent of laundered cotton and herbal shampoo. Over her shoulder I watched as Stas and Darren shook hands. "You're renting in style. Stas is very impressed."

"Oh, it's ridiculous. You'd think we could do without a luxury car for a week-long road trip. But you know Darren."

Darren and Lillian had met in law school. He was now a senior associate specializing in mergers and acquisitions at Skadden, Arps. Lillian was a defense attorney and a partner in her own firm. They had been trying to have children for a long time and for that reason, I'd put off telling Lillian I was pregnant again. But now she tentatively touched my swelling belly.

"Oh my goodness," she said. "Are you…?"

I gripped her hand in both of mine. "I am."

Tears sprang to her eyes. "That's *wonderful*," she said. "Why didn't you tell us?"

"Oh, Lily. I just wanted to wait until after the first trimester. You know how it is."

"How far along are you?"

"Thirteen weeks. I was going to tell you this weekend, honestly. I wanted to tell you in person."

"That's just so wonderful, honey. I'm so happy for you." A little abruptly, Lillian turned to peer into the backseat of our car. She kept her face averted as she lifted Clara out and made a breathless, affectionate fuss over her. "Sweetie-pie, hi! I'm so glad to see you. I missed you so much!"

Inside the house, my sister and her husband exclaimed over the dramatic fireplace and the kitchen's rustic charm. I went to the sink to refill my water bottle but when I turned the faucet, nothing happened.

"What the hell," Stas said. I stepped into the laundry alcove and tried that sink too. The water was off.

It was the Saturday of Memorial Day weekend. Stas called

the water department and got a recorded message. I called Rae and got her voicemail. Walking down our new driveway to the U-Haul, I thought about three days with no working sinks, showers, or toilets.

"Hey, what's the trouble?"

I looked up to see Jack grinning at me from the next yard.

"You look like someone pissed in your cornflakes," he said.

I told him about the water. He stepped away from his pail of plaster and wiped his hands on his pants. "Maybe I can give you a hand. Let me take a look."

He followed me back to the house, where I introduced him to everyone else. Then he disappeared into the basement. When he resurfaced a few minutes later, the water was back on.

We all exclaimed with relief. My unease of the day before was replaced by gratitude. How lucky that I'd met Jack! We invited him to grab a bagel and cream cheese from the breakfast spread on the kitchen island. He dug in without hesitation. He seemed to be in no hurry to leave.

Eventually Stas and I turned to the task of hauling boxes into different rooms while Jack lingered over his third cup of coffee, talking to Darren.

"You see, Stas," I said, as we unpacked linen and quilts and clothing in our new bedroom. "It's a good thing I met Jack after all. Otherwise we'd have no water till Tuesday."

"He really knows this house," Stas conceded.

"Listen," said Lillian when we were alone later, drinking green tea at the kitchen table. "I know you're mostly a stay-at-home mom right now, but if you're interested in a one-time paying job that you can do at your convenience, a client of mine just told me about a project that might intrigue you. It won't pay much, of course."

"What is it?"

"Well, he's blind and affiliated with all kinds of advocacy groups. Apparently one of them received an endowment for the purpose of creating an audio library of poetry."

She drew a slender hardcover from her purse. The title was *Different Hours*; the poet's name was Stephen Dunn.

"Whether or not you'd like to record for them, I think you would love this," she said. "It won a Pulitzer. Anyway, have a look at it and let me know whether you'd like to be a reader. You'd be recording all the poems for around seventy-five dollars."

I took the book without opening it. "It was nice of you to think of me, Lily."

"Do you ever think of trying out for any local theater?"

"Yeah, there are a million parts for pregnant women."

Right away, I regretted saying this. Lillian held her teacup with both hands and stared into the pale green liquid without answering.

"I'm sorry, Lil," I said after a moment. "It's just—acting is not a part of my life anymore, and I'm okay with that."

"All right."

I felt my throat tighten.

"What's that sound?" my sister asked suddenly.

"What sound?"

"Listen," she said, and then I heard it: something like a trickle of rain, but coming from inside the house. As we rose to investigate, Stas and Darren wandered up from the basement where they'd been flattening empty boxes; they had heard it too. The guest room ceiling was leaking. A steady stream of water splashed from the rafters and pooled on the floor. As I ran to get a mop and bucket, it came to me for the first time that there was no landlord to handle this, no building manager to call.

"I can't believe it. On our very first night!" I said to Stas.

"How much did we pay for that inspection? No one said anything about a leak!"

"Welcome to home ownership," my brother-in-law said.

But lying in bed a little later, I was bone-tired and deeply pleased. I loved the house. The yard had space enough for a swing set and sandbox. There was a lovely wooden side porch between the house and the garage. And come winter, a fire would blaze inside the stone hearth.

3

"How's about you haul boxes around today, and I'll spend time bonding with my niece," Darren suggested to Lillian the next morning.

"Nice try."

"C'mon, it's only fair. You had your turn at the fun job."

"Overruled."

As I set a bag of trash outside the front door, I thought—as I had many times before, and never without envy—about how Lillian and Darren spoke the same language. The jargon of the law, of American culture, the countless shared nuances of native English: they bantered and bickered and jousted and joked with nothing lost in translation. Whereas Stas and I—

"Hey, how's it going?" It was Jack, raising a hand from the next yard.

"Oh, hey," I said. "Well, there's always something, I guess." I mentioned the leak.

"I can probably help you out with that too," he said. "I've fixed a lot of ceiling leaks in my time. Let me drop by when the work day's done."

I stepped back into the house and almost collided with Stas, who was just inside the front door.

"Leda," he said, in a tone of clear reproof.

"What?"

"I don't want this guy coming over every day."

"You mean Jack?"

"That's who I mean."

"Uh…okay," I said, trying to strike just the right note between amenable and bewildered, even as I fought off a secret sense of culpability. "But, I mean…where is that coming from? Do you dislike him?"

"Well, let me put it this way. I don't ever want you to be alone with him."

"What do you mean?" I asked. "What are you worried about?"

"I don't trust him."

"Trust him how? I mean, what's he going to do? We know who he is. We know where he works."

Stas was silent.

"We know his cousin," I added.

"All right," Stas said. "You don't want to listen to me? Don't listen to me then."

He left the room and I didn't go after him.

The tension lingered all afternoon: at the hardware store where we made copies of our new keys, at IKEA where we picked up a lamp for Clara's room, at Home Depot where Stas thought someone could trim the ill-fitting marble surface of our kitchen counter.

"Can't be done here, son," a man in an orange apron told him.

"Well, where should we go?" I asked. "There's an alcove for the fridge cut into our kitchen wall, but right now the marble's overlapping it. We have our refrigerator out in the middle of the kitchen floor."

"Ma'am, I don't rightly know what to tell you. You need industrial machinery for that."

"I cannot believe it is so difficult," Stas said.

"It's not as simple as you seem to think," said another employee who'd stopped to listen. "You need a diamond-coated blade to get through that kind of stone, and you need a stream of water to cool the blade on its way through. It's a highly specialized process. Might be easier just to replace it."

A Slavic-looking man came over. Without preamble, without

a glance at the other two men, he addressed my husband directly in Russian. The two conferred a moment in their native language and then the man wrote an address on a slip of paper.

Our destination turned out to be a low-slung, windowless building in the middle of a desolate parking lot. "Look at this place," Stas said, cutting the ignition. "It looks like a mafia warehouse."

Inside were stacks of stone, tile, and marble and dozens of Russian workers. One of them had a dramatic scar stretching from his left ear to the corner of his mouth. It was he who took the slab from Stas, set it on a nearby table, and drew a tool from his belt. The task took him less than ten minutes.

In the three years I'd known my husband, I'd never heard him say a good word about anyone or anything Russian. But as he replaced the marble on the counter and eased the refrigerator into its intended space, I heard him muttering to himself.

Highly specialized process, my ass…I spent more time talking to those fucking Americans than it took that Russian guy to get it done.

It was only after Lillian and Darren had left the next day, and Stas was at work, that I opened the book of poems. It was as if, without knowing why, I'd been waiting to be alone with it. I put Clara in the Exersaucer and, hoping that would keep her busy for ten minutes, turned to a poem called *Odysseus's Secret*.

At first he thought only of home, it began.
But after a few years, like anyone on his own,
he couldn't separate what he'd chosen
from what had chosen him. Calypso,
the Lotus-eaters, Circe;
a man could forget where he lived.

He had a gift for getting in and out of trouble,
a prodigious, human gift. To survive Cyclops
and withstand the Sirens' song—
just those words survive, withstand,
in his mind became a music
he moved to and lived by.

Not halfway through the poem, I became aware of the outline of a man through the window of the front door. Jack was on the porch, a tool belt slung around his hips and a slash of dirt under his left eye. "I can take a look at that leak now, if you want," he said.

And as I rose from my chair, I felt a twinge of my previous unease. The day before, surrounded by my family and absorbed by moving in, it was easy to brush off Stas' misgiving. Today I felt the emptiness of the house at my back and the desolation of my sister's departure. Still, I couldn't think of a polite way to refuse. I showed Jack into the guest room and, to keep Clara from escaping, pulled the door shut.

"It's been a while since a girl took me into a room and closed the door," he said.

This startled me into silence for a moment. "I don't want the baby to get out," I said finally, picking her up for good measure and moving toward the window. "Not with that flight of stairs so close by. So do you see the stained part of the ceiling, above the bar? That's where the water was coming in."

He glanced at the ceiling and then back at me while Clara tugged at my shirt.

"Why are you trying to undress your mommy?" he said to her. Then to me: "Why do they do that?"

The false innocence of this question seemed to alter the air in the room. It occurred to me that Jack was between me and the door now. *Oh*, I thought. *Oh. So Stas was right about him.*

But at the moment—because I hadn't listened to Stas; because I was, in fact, alone with Jack—it seemed essential not to show alarm, essential to be calm and casual.

"She's probably hungry," I said.

"Oh…so you're still…"

"Yes."

"It always makes me feel funny. To see a woman doing that. I mean, I know it's natural and all, but still. There was a woman once, I was working on her house, and I walked in on her just after she finished feeding her baby. The baby was done drinking but she hadn't put herself away yet."

"Anyway," I said. I set Clara back down. "There's the spot where the leak was."

Slowly Jack brought his gaze around to where the water had come in. "I'd have to break into that part of the ceiling to see what's going on," he told me. "Is that all right?"

I was glad when Clara wandered toward the door, giving me a reason to follow her. So far, I wasn't afraid as much as jittery, skittish; Jack seemed more off-putting and overbearing than truly menacing. But I didn't want to prolong his visit.

"Let me call Stas," I said, reaching for my cell phone, "to make sure he won't mind."

Just mentioning Stas was a relief. It was a way to remind Jack that I had a husband: a man whose consent was needed before anything could proceed.

"Tell him to wait until I get home," Stas said immediately. "Just tell him I want to be there to look at the pipes with him."

"All right," I said gratefully. "So when do you think that might be? Around six?"

"Stas wants to get a look too," I reported after hanging up. "He's hoping you can come back later."

Jack regarded me with an expression I couldn't read. "All right," he said finally. "I'll come back when he gets home."

On the threshold of the front door, though, he turned to face me once again. "Man, where the hell have I seen you before?" he asked. "It's driving me crazy."

I lifted a shoulder as if to say *no clue*, and waited until he was out of earshot to slide the metal bolt across the door.

No sooner had he disappeared than my phone rang. It was Lillian, calling from the road. "I didn't say anything yesterday," she said, "because I didn't want to get between you and Stas. But I thought he was right, actually, about the man next door. That you shouldn't be alone with him."

I moved to the front window, feeling the first pang of real foreboding. "Yeah, I'm starting to get it," I said. "But what happened yesterday, to make you say that?"

"I don't know," she said. "I didn't like the way he was looking at you."

"Well," I said. "Okay, then. I'm on board with you guys now. Don't worry."

I folded the phone and stood holding Clara in the middle of the room.

If I repeated Jack's remarks to my husband, then Stas would turn him away when he showed up, and we would have an enemy before we'd lived here a week. Jack would be next door every day while I was home alone, and who could say what he might do? For the time being, he was essentially our neighbor.

But not telling Stas seemed tantamount to a kind of complicity with Jack. It meant keeping a secret from my husband. How had I gotten into this position?

At last I resolved to avoid any future commerce with Jack. To say hello and goodbye in passing, if I had to. Nothing more.

4

"What are you doing?" Stas asked, upon coming home to find me at the kitchen table with a microcassette recorder and the Stephen Dunn book.

I explained about the poetry project.

"Seventy-five dollars?" Stas clarified.

"Yes."

"I don't understand," he said.

"Understand what?"

"Understand why you would bother."

I glared at him. "Obviously it's not about the money."

"All right," he said. "I did not mean to make you angry."

"Well, you did."

I picked up the book and recorder, went into the bedroom and closed the door. It was twenty minutes before he knocked.

"Leda. May I come in?"

"I'm busy," I told him, not lifting my eyes from *Different Hours*.

"I came to apologize to you," he said. "Please forgive me for what I said."

"It doesn't matter," I said. "I don't care. Just, I need to concentrate on this, so could you leave and close the door behind you?"

"You are still angry. All right, I understand. I have realized that my words were insensitive. You are trying to take part in a charitable endeavor."

"Okay. I'm glad you get it now," I said, even though that wasn't it at all.

Once the door had closed behind him, I returned to the page in front of me, where I'd been midway through a poem called *Their Divorce*.

It means no one can know what goes on
In the pale trappings of bedrooms,
In anyone's secret, harrowed heart.

A little later, when I heard Jack arrive, I emerged just long enough to take Clara. Then I withdrew to her room with the excuse of putting her to bed. In the nursery, I sat in the pink armchair long after she fell asleep, distantly listening to the men confer. I heard them turning on different sources of water and finally there was the sound of our front door opening and closing.

Stas was alone in the kitchen when I finally ventured downstairs, but that didn't dispel my feeling that Jack was watching me, listening to me. I felt worn out with all the tension of the past several hours—depleted, on edge, nerves frayed. I couldn't tell whether my mounting fear of Jack was exaggerated or realistic. I felt alone with it.

"Is he gone?" I asked in a hush.

"No, he is under the house," Stas told me. "In the crawl space, looking at the plumbing system."

Under the house. Suddenly it was as if I could see this scene as it unfolded on a stage or screen: the vast house, lit from within but surrounded by darkness. The troubled wife treading lightly on the kitchen floorboards, whispering to her husband. And the workman beneath her feet, beneath the house, staring overhead: all knotted muscle and clenched teeth, mythical and bristling. A member of the underworld, bent on mutiny.

"I'm so tired," I said to Stas. "I think I'll go to bed." And I climbed the stairs to the uppermost floor.

In the morning, Stas told me that Jack had fixed the leak. That he'd waved away an offer of payment. And that he'd then put in his bid for the work on our would-be nursery. He would strip the walls, then patch them, prime them and paint them. All for only two hundred dollars.

Under the circumstances, Stas added, it was hard to turn him down. After all, he'd just done us a second favor.

"He is going to start tonight," my husband said. "But I told him not to come over until seven. I said I would go next door and get him when I am home from work."

At six, there was a knock at the door.

"Look," Jack said, filling the door frame and wiping sweat from his forehead. "I know we said seven, but I've been at it since five this morning. I'd really like to get started earlier so I can finish earlier."

I stood there at a loss for what to do. I did not see how I could tell him, *After yesterday, I've decided never to be alone with you.* I let him in, resolving to stay on the ground floor while he worked on the level below.

"I gotta sit down for a minute," he said as soon as he was in the door. He grabbed a kitchen chair. "And hey, could I trouble you for a glass of water?"

For the next forty-five minutes he complained about his boss (*that cheap back-stabbing punk-ass motherfucker*). It seemed the guy had loaned him the money for a used truck and Jack was supposed to pay it back in labor.

"Sweat equity," I said.

"What?"

"Never mind. You were saying…?"

"I thought I'd have to put in eight or nine weeks on this job. He's holding back half of my hourly but paying me half too, because I have to fuckin' eat, right? But he just keeps messing with me. The first week he paid me for seven hours a day instead of eight just because I took a lunch hour when he did. After that, I caught on and started brown-bagging it, but then he called it quits for four days when his mom had an operation. He said he wants to be on-site for every step of the job, but I know what his deal is. He didn't trust me to put in an honest day's work and keep track of my hours while he was at the hospital. I told him, *Why don't you just call me a liar to my face?* And what am I supposed to do while he's kicking back with his mom? Just fuckin' sit around with my thumb up my ass? I can't get another job for just four days. It's like he has me by the fuckin' *balls*, man."

"That does sound frustrating."

Jack sighed. "With my luck that tightwad candy-ass bastard is gonna drag this out till summer." He knocked back some water and proceeded to fill me in on his sad life story. Dad had walked out early. Mom died when he was nine. For a full week, he and his thirteen-year-old brother lived alone. Then they were placed in an abusive foster home. A few years later, Jack ran away. He'd never gone past the eighth grade in school. For all these reasons and more, he admitted to having "volatility issues."

From there, he rambled onto the topic of other bosses he'd had. The rich lady for whom he'd been a chauffeur, the one who'd propositioned him from the back of her own Rolls Royce. The bored housewife on the estate where he'd done some yard work, who wanted to get it on with both him and his girlfriend.

"Hey," he said after a while. "You know what I can't stop wondering? Where the hell have I seen you before? It's driving me up the wall."

"I don't know," I told him. "Do you get out to Portland much? Like I mentioned, we were there all last year."

"Huh," he said. "Whereabouts in Portland?"

"We were renting in the Mississippi District."

"Huh," he said again. He rubbed at his goatee. "I've done some jobs in Portland. And some drinking. But I think I seen you someplace else."

"Well, I don't know. Unless you've spent time in New York?"

"Not for a long time. I was there for a little while in the eighties. Driving a limo for this high society fashion designer chick. Now there was a wild lady."

To my relief, I heard my husband's car pull into the driveway and a moment later, he was at the door. Jack didn't miss a beat as Stas came into the kitchen. He lifted his water glass in greeting.

"Hey man, how's it going?"

Stas wasn't in the mood for pleasantries. "I have work to do, and so do you," he told Jack without smiling. As he helped Jack carry down his ladder and painting supplies, I went upstairs with Clara. I did not come down again until Jack had stripped the room of wallpaper and left, telling Stas he'd resume the job toward the end of the week.

"I told you I did not want you alone with him. Why did you let him in?"

"He said he wanted to start early so he could finish early. What was I supposed to say?"

"You didn't have to answer the door."

"I didn't know it was him!"

"Well, who else did you think it might be?"

"Besides, Stas, as soon as I even came near the door, he could see me through the window. What was I going to tell him? Sorry, there's a new rule now and I can't let you in? I don't want to offend the guy outright. I'm the one who has to see him every day."

"That's the point. *I don't want you to see him every day*."

"I don't want to see him either! But he *works next door*."

"Oh man, that sucks," Rae said. We were at the bar in the Sapphire Hotel, she with her Guinness and me with a non-alcoholic beer. "I totally get what you're going through. A few years ago, my best friend had big issues with her next-door neighbor. And it was even worse for her, because she was divorced and it was just her and her baby son. Plus the neighbor actually lived there, so it wasn't like he was going away. At least your guy will be gone soon. How much longer could that job last? A couple of weeks?"

"What issues was your friend having?"

"Oh, the usual neighbor stuff. The guy made a lot of noise, for one thing. He was a low-life redneck nut job and his yard looked like shit, which drove down the value of all the nearby homes. He'd be working on his junk cars in the driveway and blasting heavy metal during her baby's nap. In the evening, he'd set off fireworks for kicks, and he left trash around, which attracted raccoons. You get the idea. At first he was just a pain in the ass, but when she tried—nicely, mind you—to talk to him about some of these things, he became outright hostile."

"What did he do?" I was almost afraid to ask.

"Well, nothing she could actually pin on him. That was the problem. He was just smart enough to avoid that mistake. But he did plenty. Like she'd wake up in the morning and find garbage on her lawn. Or worse—sometimes he let his pit bull do his business in her yard. Once she found obscene words chalked on her driveway and another time—sorry, this is nasty—there was a bloody tampon on her front steps. And of course he only did this stuff when she wasn't home, or in the middle of the night. She couldn't prove it was him, but she knew it was. And it's like you just said. She started to dread going home. Her stomach would start hurting the minute she woke up in the morning because she was afraid of what she'd find outside her door. This was her *house*, so she could never relax. The stress was killing her. Her hair was coming in gray."

"See, that's just what I don't want. I don't want a war," I said.

"Yeah, I get it," Rae repeated. "I don't blame you."

I stared into my glass, which was nearly empty.

"You say this happened a few years ago," I said finally. "So how did your friend resolve it?"

"She moved," Rae said.

"Well, we just moved *in*," I said. "That's not an option for us."

"I know it isn't."

"The thing is, I don't know how to talk about this with Stas. If I tell Stas, it *will* be an open war."

"I hear you," Rae said. "I think most men would be the same way. My own ex, the one I mentioned to you? Forget it. I could never tell him something like this, without endangering the other guy's life. Literally."

"Well, not that Stas is violent," I said. "But there's a certain coldness in him that scares me sometimes."

This was the first time I'd admitted such a thing to another person.

"Don't get me wrong," I added quickly. "He's a wonderful husband—"

"Oh, he is," Rae broke in. "I can tell. I think Stas is great. I mean outwardly, he's all business, wants to get it done, won't bother with small talk. I admit it was hard to get a read on him at first. But over time, I got the sense that he's a really good guy."

She paused to take some money from her purse as the bartender refilled our glasses. Then she lifted her beer and knocked it against mine.

"Where did you meet him, anyway?"

5

Kaiser Tech was a start-up company in midtown Manhattan that provided computer services to small businesses. I was there as a temporary receptionist. At the time, the company was just three men and me in a very small room. Bryce was the owner. He was in his early forties and looked like a cross between a koala and a cement truck. He had graying hair combed back in waves from his forehead, a barrel chest, and limbs like hams. Marcus and Stas were the two engineers, both striking in their way. Marcus was slight of build with eyes the color of a koi pond: a startling clear green flecked with gold. Stas was tall and lean with light brown hair, and his own hazel eyes were wide and dreamy.

When I'd taken this job, it hadn't seemed promising, but I was so demoralized already that it hardly mattered. I'd just botched my first major role in a Broadway play, that of Blanche DuBois in a revival of *A Streetcar Named Desire.* The critics were unanimous in trashing me (*Leda Reeve is the weak link here…this Blanche would do better to rely on the kindness of casting agents for the afternoon soaps…painful to watch, for all the wrong reasons…shallowly rendered… lacking in conviction*). This flurry of reviews appeared the morning after our opening night, and the show closed before the end of the first week.

For many days afterward, I could not stop trembling. I trembled even while lying in bed at night. During the afternoons, curled up at one corner of my threadbare sofa, it seemed my every thought included the word *failure*, the word *finished*. I made cup after cup of tea just to have something warm to hold. I was afraid to talk to anyone I knew, even afraid to answer the phone. It felt like a matter of survival to shut down, as though maybe—if I could block out any reference to the play, shun each condolence call, never look at another newspaper—none of it would be real. If I kept my head down, put one foot in front of the other, aspired to nothing beyond my own next breath, maybe I could disappear, or turn into someone else. Answering the phone for a technology company seemed like a fine start.

The temp agency gave me an address in midtown west. Getting there involved a bus and then a subway, as well as several icy blocks on foot. The office was in a dismal part of town just south of the Port Authority, where junkies and hustlers still made up much of the street population. The building was run down, the tile in the lobby crumbling. Bryce's company was on the fourth floor, and even before I reached his threshold, I could see that the space was little more than a hole in the wall. It had industrial carpeting and the walls were cracked and stained. A row of grimy windows provided a view of the building's airshaft.

An aisle divided the office, which was otherwise partitioned into cubicles. Bryce was at the far end of the room, talking on the phone; he motioned for me to take a seat. By the near wall was one small table with a folding chair, and I could see nowhere else for a visitor to sit. But no sooner had I settled there than Stas entered the room, his arms full of computer equipment. I didn't know his name yet, of course. And he did not introduce himself. What he said, in a heavy Slavic accent, was: "Please remove yourself from this table."

I stared at him.

"Stas," Bryce said, laughing. He had just hung up the phone.

"That's fucked up. Don't mind him," he told me. "He's not trying to be rude. That's just the way he talks. He's a Siberian brute."

Stas looked taken aback but said nothing further. I rose from the table and gathered my things as Bryce waved me over. "Come on back, I'm ready now anyway." He stood and nudged his own chair toward me before seating himself on the edge of his desk.

Finally Stas spoke again. "What I said was rude?"

"That's okay," Bryce told him. "We'll buff up your act yet. All in good time. Did you know I was the headmaster of a charm school before I got into the I.T. business?"

Stas ignored this. "What would an American say?" he wanted to know.

Bryce turned to me. "Lisa. It is Lisa, isn't it?"

"Leda."

"Leda, right. Leda, what would an American say? A polite American."

I smiled gently and somewhat apologetically at Stas, hoping he wouldn't hold this little etiquette lesson against me. "I guess if I needed to get someone out of my way, I might say something like…oh…*I'm so sorry to trouble you, but I'm going to need this table.*"

"I'm sorry to…trouble you?" Stas repeated.

"Yes."

I'm sorry to trouble you, he repeated in a murmur. *I'm sorry to trouble you…* And he turned back to the jumble of equipment.

Bryce grinned broadly. "Okay, great. I'm sure you'll have a perfect phone manner and this'll be the easiest money you'll ever make. We don't have any clients yet, so the phone only rings like once an hour. The pace will pick up soon, but for now you can read a book, surf the net, do whatever you want between calls."

He explained that Marcus and Stas were in the process of building a proprietary server. When they were done, the company would sell its custom network to corporate offices. In the meantime, Bryce was placing his first few ads, and if any prospective clients called, he wanted to sound like a legitimate business.

"Now here's what I want you to say when you answer the phone. No matter how dead it is. Even if it's the only call all day. Pick up and say, *Kaiser Tech, can you hold*? Like you're super busy and juggling a bunch of customers. Make them wait for like thirty seconds before you come back and talk to them."

It would be hard to explain why I felt such a sense of consolation in that shabby room. But I did; somehow the hardscrabble space seemed to offer reprieve, deep cover, even an unlikely cheer. It was like a sheltered little cove where I could drift as mindlessly as a cork, expending no effort and incurring no censure: someone workaday and sensible, blameless and safe—someone else altogether. It had something to do with the anonymity: none of these men knew me, or knew anything of my failure. Also, they were glad I was there; this was unmistakable. It had something to do with the close, cozy quarters, the snow falling outside the windows, the space heater that Stas set beneath my desk. It had something to do with the banter, which went on all day and was comforting and enlivening, and something to do with Bryce, who was a life-force unto himself. Maybe even something to do with his disdain for the world of theater.

"I moved to New York ten years ago. Want to know how many Broadway shows I've bothered to see since then? Take a guess," he said. "It's a big, round number."

"We're going to take the world by storm," he would say. "Marcus, Stas, the day we go public, I'll step aside and let you two ring the bell at the New York Stock Exchange."

"The only question is how much time we'll need to take this thing through the roof," he'd say. "But ultimately our success is guaranteed. It's guaranteed, because I'm not going to stop until I'm done."

"It's a hundred and fifteen fucking degrees," he'd say, "and we have the only swimming pool in town."

After I'd been there two weeks, Bryce took me aside. "I have an idea for you," he said. "Not just an idea, but a proposition. Not just a proposition, but a one-time opportunity. An opportunity that will *alter your destiny*."

By now I was used to outsized statements from Bryce and my only response was to smile faintly, patiently.

"I want you to stay on and help me build this company," Bryce continued. "I want you to sell the system for me."

I knew what this really meant; he'd touched on it a few times before. He wanted me to canvass the area businesses. I pictured myself going door to door like an Avon Lady. I imagined other receptionists, girls in their early twenties, whose job it would be to toss me out on my ass.

"Bryce, that's very generous of you," I told him. "But I can't."

"Why not? You'd be unstoppable, a star. I knew it the moment you stepped over the threshold."

"I don't know anything about computer networks."

"That's perfect! That's the best part. I don't want some tech-head going around for me. You don't have to know anything. You just need a few buzz words to throw at these people and you need to understand the business model. These guys are lawyers, accountants, realtors…they don't know the first thing, don't even know what questions to ask. You'll be with me the first twenty times; you'll listen, absorb the drill, learn your lines. You're an actress, for Christ's sake. It'll be the most natural thing in the world for you."

"Well, but that's the thing, Bryce. I do like to think of myself as an actress. I have to go to auditions and if I'm offered work, I need to be able to take it." This was something I was still telling myself, though I hadn't been to an audition in weeks.

"Fine. So stay an actress. No one's asking you to give up your ...career. I'm just saying, why don't you take a break? Take three months. What's three months in the big picture? Make some money, take the pressure off. Think of it like an acting exercise."

"Bryce. I'm flattered—"

"Stop. Save it. Don't answer right now—just think about it. Think about giving me three short months. No, forget that: give me *one* month. If you hate it after a month, you'll quit. No hard feelings. In the meantime, you'll make a pile of cash."

Before I left for the day, he gave me the outline of a payment plan. "First, I'll give you three thousand as a base, just for going out there every day. On top of that, you'll make fifty bucks for each appointment you set. That's not the real money, but even that'll add up. Make two appointments a day—you've got eight hours to do it, so how can you fail?—and that's another two grand a month. But where you'll make a killing is the five hundred I'll pay you for every customer you find who ends up signing.

"So let's do a little math, shall we? Two appointments a day is ten a week, right? So let's say I can only sign one client out of five. That's an *extremely conservative* estimate, my track record is way better than that, but I'm low-balling it right now so you don't think I'm leading you down some fantasy path. If I can't sign one in five, I'm not Bryce Kaiser. Stas? Marcus? You guys are my witnesses. If I can't sign one in five, I'll eat my shorts. So that's two signed clients a week, which would yield, altogether...we're talking the *worst-case scenario* here...a total of nine thousand a month for you. Have you ever made nine thousand dollars a month? That's more than a hundred grand a year. Not bad for a temp receptionist, right?"

None of Bryce's other employees ever experienced this kind of largesse. Bryce believed in stopping at nothing to motivate his sales force. Otherwise he liked his workers marginal and desperate. He wanted them to need their jobs more than they did their sanity or pride. He hired immigrants awaiting their visas, middle-aged men languishing in the wake of layoffs, even an ex-convict or two. Stas fit this profile perfectly at first, and Bryce started him off at seven dollars an hour, twelve to twenty hours a day, six to seven days a week. His hourly wage was not adjusted in any way for overtime.

During the four-day transit strike that year, Stas didn't go home at night. He slept in his office chair and shaved in the men's room. He pretended to consider joining the gym across the street to get a free trial membership. He showered there and marveled that Americans paid money to run on treadmills like rats on a wheel.

I got to know Stas slowly, and over time I learned his history. He'd come to America seven years earlier, in June of 1998, at the age of seventeen. His plan was to study English all summer at SUNY Purchase, then stay on for the academic year as an exchange student. But by August, the Russian economy had collapsed and his parents could no longer afford his tuition.

Stas never once considered going home.

He moved into the local YMCA and got a job as a busboy at the local diner. The free meal employees were allowed to eat before each shift was his one meal of the day. He filled his pockets with the thimble-sized creamers served with the coffee. Every few hours, he went to the men's room and knocked them back like shots. Sometimes he wrapped half-eaten steaks and brought them back to his room.

Once, friendless and flat broke between jobs, he went a full week without eating at all: seven days of taking in nothing but water. On the eighth day, in a jacket he unearthed from the bottom of his duffel bag, he found a five dollar bill. He walked out of the hostel and across the street to the little Chinese take-out joint, where he ordered a whole chicken and devoured it within minutes. Then he wrapped up the stripped carcass, brought it back to the Y, boiled the bones and ate those too.

Afterward, still ravenous, he could not stop himself from considering all the better ways he might have used those five dollars. He might have bought several boxes of pasta, or a few dozen eggs, or a loaf of bread and a jar of peanut butter—sustenance that could be stretched over several days rather than wolfed down in one sitting. But by the time this occurred to him, it was too late. The money had been spent.

I gave Rae these details during our second round at the bar.

"That takes a pair of *balls*," she said. "To just come over by himself like that, and make his own way. Has he seen his parents since?"

"No," I said. "Never. Not for ten years."

"That's *incredible*."

"Yes."

It was in fact the aspect of my husband I found most fascinating—the account of his early days in America with no English, no money, no contacts, no help, and then his eventual migration to Manhattan, to real opportunity. Stas said the word *opportunity* with something like reverence. He named it as the reason he came to America in the first place.

When he reached the big city, he took a cheap apartment share in Inwood. His roommate was Dmitri, a young man from Moscow. The two made a pact that was never violated: a pact not to speak Russian to each other.

"How did you do it?" It was a question I asked over and over.

"Well, we had a Russian-English dictionary, so we could look up words we didn't know. It wasn't perfect, but it was enough to be understood."

"No, I mean, how could you stand it? If I had to work in another country and I had an American roommate, I'd be so relieved to talk freely at the end of the day."

"We wanted to forget Russian altogether," he said quietly. "We wanted to speak English."

"That's intense," Rae said. "Something must have happened to him there."

"I think so too," I told her. "But I don't really know." Beyond the bare outline of his survival in the U.S., Stas didn't talk about his past.

"So," she said. "How did you two go from being co-workers to hooking up?"

I glanced at the clock above the bar, which revealed that it was almost Clara's bedtime. I always nursed her to sleep.

"Oh Rae, I can't believe it's nine o'clock already," I said. "I'd love to tell you that story, but I have to wait till next time."

"Here's what I'll do," she told me. "I can't believe I forgot your receipts. But tomorrow I'm showing a house in your neighborhood—late in the day, like at four or five. I'll bring you the receipts when I'm done. If you're not home, I'll just leave them in your mailbox. But if you're around and you feel like it, you can tell me more."

6

The following morning, after dropping Clara off at preschool, I knew Jack would show up the moment I returned to the house. In the parking lot, at the classroom door, at the wheel of my car, I felt him waiting for me. It felt personal, as if I had revealed myself as his rightful quarry. This thought kept me at the nearest coffeehouse for an hour, lingering over a local newspaper, but there was no way to avoid going home all day.

Sure enough, a minute or so after I stepped into the house, there was a hearty knock at the door. My car was in the driveway and he'd probably seen me as well. It didn't matter; I wouldn't answer. *I can say the baby kept me up all night and I fell back to sleep*, I thought. *Or I can say I was in the shower.* He rang the doorbell, knocked some more, then rang again. After many long minutes, he seemed to give up. But now it was dangerous to go downstairs, where I could be seen through several windows. The curtains were open and I'd have to step into plain sight to close them. I was avoiding my own living room, my own kitchen, afraid to get a glass of water or unload the dishwasher. I was hiding in my own house.

I busied myself with chores I might not ordinarily have bothered with, like making the beds and sorting out a large plastic bag of Clara's toys: puzzle pieces, doll house furniture, magnetic letters, plastic blocks. An image came to me: myself in third grade, reading in the library during recess rather than brave the blacktop where certain girls were likely to torment me. I didn't mind being inside with a good book; it might even be fair to say I preferred it. But sitting alone at the table, brow furrowed in a show of concentration, I felt secretly compromised, impotent.

At noon, I resolved to go out for groceries. Jack materialized the moment I stepped onto the side porch. He was holding a stack of little cardboard boxes.

"Hey, I knocked on your door earlier with these, but no one answered," he said.

"Really? I'm sorry," I told him. "I didn't hear anything. I must have been in the shower."

"Your husband mentioned your rodent problem in the garage. I had a bunch of these left over from a job last year, so I thought I'd bring 'em by," he said. "Your garage was open, so I scattered a few of 'em around to get you started." He held out the boxes and I saw that they were glue traps.

It took all my self-control not to recoil. I managed to smile at Jack, and thank him, and endure several more minutes of small talk about the progress on the house next door. I did not betray my horror of glue traps or the fact that the ones he'd just given me were going straight into the kitchen trash compactor. As soon as he was out of sight, I stepped into the garage for the ones he'd already left there. I was holding my breath as I scanned the dim interior. *Please, they haven't been here for more than a few hours; please let all of them be empty.*

The one in the near corner was untouched, as were the two along the opposite wall. I went around the periphery picking them up, being careful not to touch the glue pads. I'd heard stories of people losing skin to the sticky part, and once in a veterinarian's office, I'd seen a dog with a trap glued to its paw.

There were two more along the back wall. The first was empty, but the struggling form of a mouse was flattened against the other one.

I stood very still, knuckles pressed to my mouth.

Nausea came easily to me throughout my pregnancies, and a wave of it broke over me then. My objection to mouse traps in the garage—for that matter, my objection to killing just about anything (I would coax a spider onto a piece of paper and set it outside rather than step on it)—was an ongoing source of amusement and annoyance to Stas. I wouldn't let him sprinkle weed killer in the yard for fear of poisoning a squirrel or bird, and I cringed at every instance of road kill we saw from the car. I couldn't bring myself now to really look at this mouse, any more than I could bear to really think about glue traps. What could be worse than stepping onto a surface that held you fast at every point of contact? I knew how glue traps worked: the more the mouse twisted in an effort to escape, the more contorted and stuck it would become. Finally it would lie there panting, its body rippling in panic. The worst part was, the trap would hold it in place but death might not come for days. There was nothing to finish it off besides slow starvation.

I'm sorry, I whispered to the mouse. Tears came into my eyes. *Oh you poor little thing, I'm so sorry.* If only I'd come to the door when Jack knocked: then this never would have happened.

When I called Stas at work, it was quarter to noon. I was so distraught he could barely make out what I was saying, but gradually he understood that if he left the office that minute and drove straight home, he would have just enough time to put the mouse out of its misery and still make his one o'clock meeting. It would mean sacrificing his lunch hour.

"This can wait until I get home," he told me.

"No, it can't! Stas, *please.* If you never do another thing for me. That poor mouse is *suffering.*"

"It's vermin. It's probably carrying all kinds of diseases."

"It's an innocent animal! *Glue traps are torture.*"

"This is crazy. Woman," he said. No one besides my husband had ever called me "woman" without irony. "Why are you so crazy about every filthy creature?"

"Stas, please," I sobbed.

"All *right*. All right! Listen to me, don't touch the mouse or the trap. Leave it where it is and go to the store. You were going to the store, right?"

"Yes," I sniffled.

"So go away while I kill the mouse. It will be better for you this way," he said. "And listen, while you are there, get me some smoked fish."

"Oh, honey," Rae said. "This sounds bad." She was here with our fuel receipts and I was desperate for her counsel.

"What I can't tell is whether he was taking revenge. Against me. For not answering the door. Maybe that sounds paranoid, but—"

"It doesn't at all," Rae interrupted. "The man is harassing you, and I'm sure he's getting off on it. I know that type. They can smell your fear."

"That's how I feel—like he's toying with me." Walking a deliberate line between neighborly solicitude and ruthless intrusion.

"What does Stas say about all this?"

"He has no idea, really. I mean, he thinks Jack's a nuisance and a pain in the ass. But I haven't told him the half of it. And at this point, if I go there, I'll have to admit that I've kept it from him all this time."

"Maybe you should tell him anyway," Rae said. "You know? I mean, he's your husband."

I considered this in silence, staring down at the table.

"And speaking of Stas," she said, "I still want to hear how you two got it on."

7

Stas liked to say he fell in love with me the day I showed up at Kaiser Tech. And it was true that I'd been aware of a puppyish crush on his part, something I regarded with tender amusement when I considered it at all. He was nine years younger than me and spoke broken English. He lived in Inwood, with a roommate.

Still, he managed to conduct a steady and strenuous courtship within our working relationship. If I promised a client we could install their new network right away, Stas would stay up all night getting it done. When I dropped a gold earring down the drain of the bathroom sink, Stas took apart the pipes and recovered it for me. And he wouldn't let me be alone in the office after dark. "This building is not safe," he said. "And the neighborhood is not safe either." On such evenings, he stayed at his own desk, entering data and adjusting spreadsheets until I was ready to go. Sometimes we had dinner delivered, and afterward he would walk me home.

One night everyone from the office went for drinks, and Marcus left after the second round. Bryce, Stas and I moved on to another bar, which was across from a midtown strip joint. "Ever been inside one of those places, Stas?" asked Bryce.

Stas said no.

"I'll have to show you the ropes, then. Some other time. Not tonight," he said. "Tonight I need to talk with Leda about our strategy for signing this hedge fund. We're sitting down with them in the morning."

It was a dismissal, but I could see that Stas did not want to go. He put on his jacket but remained at the table, nursing what was left of his drink.

"Seriously, Stas. It's past your bedtime," Bryce said. "Get out of here so Leda and I can review the battle plan."

There was an awkward moment where Stas sat without moving. Then slowly he stood up, knocking back the dregs of the martini Bryce had ordered for him.

"We'll see you tomorrow," Bryce said.

Stas touched his brow in a drunken salute before making his way to the door. We watched him go.

"That poor son of a bitch is in love with you," Bryce told me.

"He's just a young pup," I said. "He'll get over it."

"My favorite kind of woman," Bryce said with appreciation. "Heartless."

He nodded at the neon girlie palace framed by the bar's front window. "So what do you say we have our next round across the street?"

"A little silicone with our strategy meeting?"

"Come on, you'll love it, the girls are super fucking hot."

As we stumbled across Ninth Avenue and made our way along the sidewalk, I caught sight of Stas half a block behind us, lingering outside a branch office of Off-Track Betting.

"Hey," I said to Bryce. "Stas is following us."

"He just wants to see where we're going, I bet," Bryce told me, pushing open the smoked-glass door of the club. "He won't come in. He can't afford even the cover at a place like this."

Alcohol had left me careless, but some slight misgiving nagged at me as we climbed the stairs. I glanced back over my shoulder.

"Don't worry," Bryce added. "He's not the type to talk. Besides, who's he gonna tell? Marcus? Fuck that guy, I don't care what he thinks."

For the next couple of hours, I made out with Bryce and a girl who called herself Calypso. But afterward, even as drunk as I was, I wouldn't let him get into the taxi he'd hailed for me. With Bryce, any long-term relationship—whatever its nature—was like a game of chess, and having sex with him would have been like sacrificing my queen.

"Leda," he pleaded. "Just let me share the cab."

"There are plenty of cabs. Get your own."

"Come on. I'll have the guy drop you off first. I swear I won't try to come in."

"You live uptown, and I'm on the lower east side," I said. "It makes no sense."

I got into the back of the taxi and tried to pull the door shut behind me. Bryce held it and clambered in after me. Hastily, I slid across the seat, opened the other door and let myself out. Bryce followed while the driver cursed in his native language.

Suddenly Stas materialized between us. "Enough," he said to Bryce. His face was very pale and bathed in a light sweat. He was swaying on his feet, as if the past few hours hadn't sobered him at all. "This is enough. Leave her alone."

Bryce burst out laughing. "Stas, you madman, where the fuck did you come from? Where's your white fucking horse? Take it from me, my young friend—this fair maiden doesn't need your help."

"Enough, sir," Stas repeated. "This is not proper conduct for a man in your position."

While Bryce bellowed with mirth, I got back into the cab. The driver muttered with relief as I told him my address. As we pulled away from the curb, I couldn't resist a glance through the rear windshield. Bryce had thrown an arm around Stas and was jostling him toward yet another bar.

*

Had I been any younger, Bryce would have been a perfect candidate for my emotional investment: married (for the third time) with children, prone to cocaine and alcohol abuse, just this side of sociopathic. But as it was, I was making myself go out on dates with ostensibly reasonable prospects: men I met at parties or through friends or over the internet. The next morning, I'd entertain the office with the discouraging things they'd said or done. I'd tell everyone that this or that man hated cats, wore spiced cologne, was rude to the waitress. I'd report that he answered his cell phone during dinner, or that when we reached his car, he opened his own door first.

"Why don't you just marry Stas?" Bryce would joke in front of everyone. "He's crazy about you and he's got a good job."

Stas never reacted to these statements, never voiced agreement or denial or resentment or chagrin. His expression did not change as he studied his computer screen or stripped a modem for parts.

"Isn't that right, Stas?" Bryce would press.

"Right," he'd say absently, as if tossing a dog a bone so it would go away.

I'd been working at Kaiser Tech for nearly a year when my home computer crashed and Stas came over to fix it. This meant taking a series of trains and buses all the way from Inwood to the lower east side on his first day off in three weeks. Though he had walked me home from the office many times before, he'd never been inside my building. This was partly because I didn't want to lead him on, and partly because I was pained by the state of my apartment.

I lived in a one-bedroom apartment, and everything in it was falling apart. The kitchen faucet sprayed rivulets in all directions. The bathroom door scraped hard against the floor and the lock refused to catch. The light fixture above my bed had a burned-out bulb that seemed welded into its socket. The built-in ladder to my loft bed had a broken bottom rung.

Stas installed a program that would defragment my hard drive and get rid of its viruses. "Just let it run," he told me. "Don't touch anything for half an hour. I have a few things to do but I will come back when it is finished."

I promised not to touch the computer while he was gone. I was cleaning out the bedroom closet anyway, a project I'd started so I wouldn't be in his way. For this reason, I heard but did not see him when he walked back in, and for the next hour or so I managed to be unaware that he was fixing everything in my apartment.

"Stas," I said in amazement when, along with my restored computer, he showed me the working light and faucet and ladder and door. "Is everyone right? Should I stop dating these crazy men and marry you?"

It wasn't a real question. But Stas looked back at me with a level intensity that bordered on reproach. "Yes," he said, and there was nothing light or flippant in his voice. "Yes, you should."

I knew it would be terrible to let myself laugh.

"Oh Stas. Honey. Listen to me. I wasn't being serious. Look, you're a very attractive young man. But I'm nine years older than you, and I want children. I mean, I want to get pregnant *soon*. You're not ready for that, are you? And do you really think you'd be faithful to a middle-aged lady when you're in your prime?"

My tone was light and tender, cajoling, consoling. But Stas stared straight into my eyes with an expression that made him look, for the first time, like a man instead of a boy. And when he spoke, his gaze did not waver. "*Yes*," he said again. "Yes, I would."

It was then that I felt it, the first twinge of attraction to him, like the flutter of a butterfly in a nearly airless jar. But it was only a twinge, and I dismissed it.

The next morning, he went to Chicago.

8

"I love this," Rae said. "I love this story! Stas is the man!"

We were at the kitchen table with teacups and a pot of Darjeeling between us. I felt safe with Rae in the room. Still, when I caught sight of Jack through the window, hurling a paint-splattered tarp into the back of his truck, I felt myself cringing. Rae followed my gaze to the neighboring driveway. She nodded in his direction.

"That's the guy?"

"Shh," I cautioned.

"Leda," she laughed. "He can't hear me!"

I felt my face get hot. "I know. You're right. Of course he can't. I don't know why I said that."

"It's okay," she said, after a moment. She reached over and touched my hand. "You're just spooked."

Jack turned in my direction. He seemed to be looking straight at me, something that wasn't lost on Rae. She held my eyes as she said, "Tell Stas that he's bothering you. I trust Stas. Based on everything you just told me." And then, as if to steady me, she asked, "Why did he go to Chicago?"

Stas went to Chicago on his first business trip to wire an important client's satellite office. He was away for five days and it was a revelation. I was amazed that I missed him, that it felt as if a vital part of the work atmosphere was gone. Until then, I'd thought that Bryce alone created the frisson in the office, but now I understood that Stas supplied an essential part of it as well.

On the third day of his absence, I heard Bryce on the phone.

"Stas, man, you're making me proud, these guys tell me you've been the consummate professional. How do you think it's going?"

Then: "Good. Perfect. I'm sure you're taking great care of these people. Now listen, did Lara's friend call you…? She did? So you're seeing her?"

Lara was Bryce's wife. I put down the press kit I was assembling.

"Tomorrow night! All right, you lucky dog, you're going to thank me for this," Bryce was saying. "My young friend, let me tell you…that woman…is *smoking*. Hot as a fucking pistol. The type that'll sing for her supper and get breakfast in the bargain, if you know what I mean. Take her somewhere nice, you can add it to your tab for doing such a kick-ass job out there."

When Bryce hung up, I turned to the press kit once again. "So what was that all about?" I asked, trying for an offhand tone.

"What do you mean?"

"It sounds like you're hooking Stas up with some kind of prostitute."

"Prostitute? Come on. Not at all. She's a friend of my wife's."

"Okay, but you were basically saying he could expect to get laid."

"Look, she's a fun-loving lady, what's the harm in that? Plus, Stas is just her type. She likes them tall, young, foreign, boyish. What do you care, anyway?"

"It's not that I *care*. I just think it's a bit much. He's only a kid, for Christ's sake."

Bryce broke into a sudden grin.

"Leda, listen to you!"

"What?"

"You're jealous!"

"Oh, *come on.*"

"Christ on a sidecar. I never thought I'd see the day. Marcus, would you get this? Leda's jealous!"

"Bryce, shut up, you're so ridiculous."

A couple of hours later, unable to think of anything else, I typed the only question I could bring myself to ask—*How do you like Chicago?*—into a text message to Stas.

A moment later came the vibration of his reply and I clutched at the phone with both hands, as if the device itself were what I couldn't afford to lose.

I like it very much, he had written back. *It is a marvelous city.*

Then a moment later, he added: *You sent me here, in a way.*

I knew what he meant: that I'd signed the firm he was there to service. But I couldn't help reading another meaning into his words: that I'd sent him away by rejecting his love. What was there to hold him in New York? A room in Inwood; slave wages for work that was never done; a woman who wouldn't take him seriously. He was rootless, he could go anywhere.

The next night, the night I knew he was with Lara's friend, I couldn't eat dinner. I couldn't eat at all, in fact, or do anything besides picture Stas in her bed. I saw him going home with her and never wanting to leave. I imagined him calling Bryce, saying he'd be staying in Chicago, thanks for everything, good luck and goodbye. It would be my fault for failing to value him, for not recognizing his worth while he was mine for the taking.

Before it was even fully dark, I climbed into my loft bed and wrapped both arms around my pillow. I was holding my phone and trying to decide whether to call Stas. I had never called him for reasons unrelated to work, never called him in the evening at all. He would be with her right now, in some loud, crowded place; even if he could hear his phone ring, he'd be surrounded by other people. There would be no way to have a real conversation. And anyway, what would I say?

Could this really be happening, could this be me? Smoldering, suffering, over *Stas*? I felt tears sliding out of my eyes, staining the pillow. I was still in my work clothes, a fitted blouse and houndstooth skirt suit. I was thirty-four and pathetic.

Finally, at half past midnight, I dialed his number in a kind of frenzy. It was eleven-thirty in Chicago, late enough for his sleeping arrangements to have been decided. Surely if he was with her, he just wouldn't answer. I lay back against the bank of pillows with the phone held tight to my ear and one hand shielding my eyes.

"Leda?"

His voice came through clearly, with no din in the background. That didn't mean he was alone, of course. He could be at her house already. Or she might be in his room.

"Stas—" I felt my voice catch.

"Yes, Leda?"

"Stas, where are you?"

"I am in my hotel room. Why do you ask? Is the client having a problem?"

"Are you alone right now?"

"Yes, of course." Then, again: "Why do you ask?"

I exhaled as quietly as I could. "I just—I didn't want to interrupt you if you were with someone."

"Who would I be with here?"

I said, a little shakily, "Bryce mentioned some woman you were going out with tonight."

"Oh yes," he said. "Antonia. I met her earlier."

I didn't want to ask, but I couldn't stop myself. "What was she like?"

"She was nice," Stas said. "She bought me a shirt."

"A shirt?"

"We were walking on the street and she saw it in the window of a store. She asked whether I owned any silk shirts, and I said no. Then she said that every young man should have at least one. So she bought it for me."

"That was generous of her," I said uncertainly. "What...what color is it?"

"It is an unusual color," he said. "In the store it looked silver but when we were again on the street it was more like blue. I must say the material is very nice." He paused. "Leda, is something the matter?"

Overcome with self-consciousness, I spoke in a rush. "I just—listening to Bryce, I thought—well, I was sure she was going to invite you home with her."

"Oh yes. She did invite me," Stas said.

"She did?"

"Yes. But I apologized and told her I was tired."

"Oh," I said. "Well. Was she upset?" It seemed I was compelled to pepper him with senseless questions. As though maybe—if I didn't allow the slightest lull in the conversation, if I created a distracting enough barrage—he'd forget to wonder what this was all about.

"It is possible," he told me. "But how could I spend the night with a woman I have only just met?"

I closed my eyes and felt myself smiling. "Maybe she thought that if you felt that way, you shouldn't have accepted the shirt," I told him.

"The shirt?" He sounded surprised. "With the shirt she did not leave me a choice."

"What an innocent." Rae was laughing.

"Guileless. Yes."

"So then what? Did you ever tell him why you were calling?"

"All I said was that I needed to tell him something. He was

flying back on a Friday evening. So I asked if we could have dinner at some point during the weekend. I named a pizza place we liked on the upper west side."

"Ah," said Rae. "And he said yes?"

He came straight from the airport, his duffel bag on his shoulder.

9

After Rae left, I cleared the teacups from the table. A light rain was falling outside and the radio was playing low. I was clench-jawed and awash with all the nostalgia I'd dredged up over the past hour, newly bewildered by the sight of our front lawn through the kitchen window. What were we doing here?

When we left Kaiser Tech to come west, Bryce told us that we'd regret it—that we were making the biggest mistake of our lives. That if it weren't for him, I'd still be answering the phone somewhere; that Stas would still be a busboy. He said that within a year or two, he—Bryce—would be on the cover of *Fortune* magazine, and we would be nowhere. He told us we were ingrates and losers. We still missed him sometimes.

Bryce had been right about one thing—I made a lot of money at Kaiser Tech. Eventually even Stas made a fair amount of money. Once we had a captive client base, Stas came up with the idea of providing whatever peripheral equipment our customers wanted. If a client was in need of a printer, an extra monitor, a fax modem, Stas would order and install it and keep half of the fee. By the time we left the company, we had enough to live on for a few years.

This was fortunate, since I was visibly pregnant and therefore unemployable when we arrived in Portland. I didn't work during my third trimester and I stayed home with Clara through-out the first year of her life. I walked around the neighborhood with the baby in a stroller or a sling. I was slow to lose the baby weight and wore maternity clothes for many months after giving birth.

In self-imposed exile from the world of theater and film, I

had no life to inhabit but my own. It was like walking around in an invisible straitjacket. Was this how other people felt all the time?

Acting had made life so much more exciting. It was a chance to be other people and at the same time a way to access facets of myself I'd find hard to confront head-on. As Blanche DuBois, I could be aging, desperate and pathetic; it was safe to let myself feel those emotions beneath the cover of a role.

Having a very young child was both a distraction from, and a constant reminder of, the fact that my career was hopelessly derailed. There was at once no time and nothing but time. Nearly every waking moment was taken by the baby: by the need to feed or change or soothe or amuse her. I took her to a music class and an infant massage class and the children's museum and the zoo. I took her to play spaces and our neighborhood Mommy and Me sessions and the local swimming pool. As countless other mothers had advised me, I napped when she napped. In bookstores and coffeehouses and store-front windows, I resolutely ignored flyers for local plays and audition calls for independent films.

Stas' career, on the other hand, had taken a turn for the better. Intel's working day began at nine and ended at five. He was actually making more money working forty hours a week in Portland than he had while working around the clock in New York, and now he had paid vacation days and full benefits and a fifty percent adjustment for overtime. He bought a used Hyundai and then a new Civic.

Then since Oregon, unlike New York, did not require a license, he also bought several guns: a revolver, a shotgun, and finally, startlingly, an automatic rifle. He added these firearms along with many boxes of ammo to his strange collection of military gear and body armor. Often he went to a local shooting range and came back with bullet-riddled paper targets.

What was all this about? He liked it. That was all I could ever get him to say.

Different Hours was lying on the kitchen table. I opened it to a random page and read these words:

> *I was elsewhere, on my way to a party.*
> *On arrival, everyone was sure to be carrying*
> *a piece of the awful world with him.*
>
> *Not one of us wouldn't be smiling.*
> *There'd be drinks, irony, hidden animosities.*
> *Something large would be missing.*
> *But most of us would understand*
> *something large would always be missing.*

The next afternoon, when I left the house, Jack waylaid me in the driveway.

"Hey, I've got a great deal for you," he told me. "I know you guys want to rip up some carpet and put down wood."

"In the future. Yes," I said. "But as it turns out, we can't really afford that right now."

"Well, see, that's why I'm telling you about this. Because you said you want to cut corners where you can, and I've got a whole pile of great wood left over from this job. It's incredible quality, imported from Japan. Dark cherry, like you've never seen in your life. Top of the line, and I can sell it to you cheap. Real cheap—like less than half of what you'd pay anywhere else."

I made myself meet his eyes. "Jack, that's so nice of you, and I appreciate the thought," I told him. "But like I said, I just don't think we'll be tackling the floor project anytime soon."

"My thinking on this, though," he persisted, "is even if you hold out a while on the installation, you won't want to pass up a deal like this. You should grab the wood at this price and keep it in the garage until you're ready. I mean, honestly? You'll probably save hundreds of dollars this way."

"Well again, it's a very kind offer," I said. "I'll be sure to run the idea by Stas." It sickened me to hear myself equivocating, placating. Playing the wife who couldn't make a decision by herself.

"That's cool," Jack said, clearly disappointed. "But hey, at least come and look at it. You won't believe the color."

"It sounds beautiful, but I don't have time right now," I told him. "I'm actually running a little late to pick up Clara." This wasn't true. I was bringing our Hyundai to a mechanic in Portland, who would keep it until the next evening. The shop would loan me another car for the duration, but I didn't want Jack to know that.

"It'll just take a second."

"I can't."

"All right, all right. When you come back, then." He eased himself away from the car, then stopped short as I was opening the door.

"Oh, man," he said suddenly.

I looked up at him. His jaw had slackened and his mouth was slightly open.

"What?" I stood just behind the car's open door as if to shield myself from whatever he would say.

"Ohhhh...*man.*"

I waited.

"Now I know where I seen you before. Oh, man!"

I felt sweat breaking out under my arms and I was overcome by a nameless dread.

"*Payback*. You're the girl in *Payback*! Ain't you?"

10

Unbelievable. It was unbelievable. Nothing he said could have been more alarming. Of everything I'd done in my nearly invisible career, the starring role in *Payback* had to be the most obscure—as well as the most compromising. It was the tawdriest part I had ever played.

In *Payback*, which could only be described as soft porn, I played Jenny J., a gold-digging bimbo who's made a fortune moving from one hapless rich man to the next. At the movie's outset, she's married to an elderly millionaire. She takes a young man as a lover, a hard-muscled stud into whips and chains. By the movie's conclusion, the husband is dead, but Jenny's inheritance has been turned over to her lover, to whom she is now enslaved. She's been brought down, reduced to a maid and a plaything. She does all the housework around the lover's new mansion wearing nothing but a leather harness. She sleeps in chains and is forced to watch her master have sex with other women.

It was hard to believe that Jack had identified me. I would have thought myself unrecognizable. When that movie was made, I was seventeen years younger and forty pounds lighter. Also, my dark hair had been platinum then, and tinted contacts had made my hazel eyes blue.

"Oh, that." I tried to laugh. "That was so long ago I can barely remember it."

"Are you shittin' me? It's a classic. I've watched it so many times it's a wonder the tape ain't wore out. Oh man, I can't believe I'm standing here talking to you! You don't know how many nights I've gotten off on that flick. If you'll excuse my saying."

Breathe, I told myself.

"Hey," he said. "If you don't mind my asking, what's your husband think of that movie?"

I could have lied. Could've said, *He doesn't think about it much one way or the other.* But what if he said something to Stas? Something jocular and congratulatory? What if he raised a beer in drunken homage one evening? I couldn't take that chance.

"He doesn't know about it," I said finally.

"Oh, is that how it is? Well, hey—I understand."

"I mean, it's just never come up."

"Yeah, I hear you. Well, don't worry. Your little secret's safe with me. I promise."

Nausea rose in my throat. "It's not really a *secret*. It's just, there's been no reason to mention it."

"I get it, honey. You don't need to explain nothing to me. A girl's gotta do things for her career sometimes. I know how it is."

I looked away, afraid he would see how much I hated him.

"Don't get me wrong," he continued. "It's a smokin' movie. I don't think you got a thing to apologize for. But I can see how I might feel funny about it, if it was my wife."

After driving around the corner and out of sight of our house, I had to pull over to the shoulder of the road. My hands were trembling so violently I was afraid to drive. It was as if I'd pursued every possible avenue away from my former self: trading the acting life for the business arena; the east coast for the west; the limitless, glittering city for a small and unassuming town; the life of a free spirit for marriage and motherhood. But Jack had recognized me; he had found me. He knew things about me that my own husband didn't know, and for that matter, it was as if he alone could see me for what I was: hopelessly compromised, desperate, dissembling, best suited for a fifth-rate blue movie.

If I told Stas about *Payback*, what would he think? It was possible that he would be appalled. In some ways, he was very concerned with propriety: he often remarked that this or that would not be proper. For instance, though he often saw other men wearing what appeared to be pajama pants in public (sometimes they really were pajamas; sometimes they were scrubs), he refused to wear his own even to the curb while putting out the trash. ("This would not be proper.") On the other hand, I knew he saw me as a little scandalous, a little wild—and that, to him, this lent me some measure of glamour. My evening at the strip joint with Bryce, for instance, hadn't diminished his crush on me, and perhaps it had even done the opposite. It was possible that Stas would secretly enjoy such a movie but hate the idea of other men watching it. I realized I had no idea what he would think or how he would feel.

But the idea of sharing a secret with Jack—any secret, but especially this one—made me feel so ill that after I'd dropped off the Hyundai and gotten Clara, I had to bring a pillow into her room and lie on the floor while she played.

"Is that the loaner car?" Stas asked. "That Pontiac?"

He was just in from work, and he was referring to the dark blue sedan parked on the street out front. We were in the kitchen, and I was trying hard not to reveal any hint of my own distress.

"Yes."

"Well, why did you put it there instead of the driveway or garage?"

I'd anticipated this, and had a ready explanation. "Earlier today, Jack's boss came by and asked if he could put a dumpster in our driveway for a couple of hours."

"A dumpster?"

"I guess he had more trash than he could haul away in his flatbed. It was still there when I got back."

"Oh. Okay."

It was a risk, saying this, but just a slight one. I could not see any reason for Stas to ever bring it up with Jack's boss. And I knew Stas wouldn't care enough about the Pontiac to bother moving it. He liked to have our own cars in the garage at night, but the Pontiac was old and belonged to someone else; we weren't even formally liable for it.

The real reason I'd parked at the curb was to throw Jack off. He wouldn't know the car was mine, and tomorrow it would look like I wasn't home. The idea of a full day's reprieve from Jack was worth a meaningless lie to Stas.

Rae's question at the bar came back to me: *how much longer could that job last?* The only real exchange I'd had with the boss had to do with just how long he and Jack might be there.

"So how soon do you think we can expect new neighbors?" I'd asked, as if looking forward to meeting a nice family instead of counting the days until the work was done and Jack was gone.

"Oh, you know what they say," the boss said cheerfully. "There are three speeds in construction: slow, dead and reverse." He chuckled, saying this. "We've got a ways to go yet."

I thought of calling Rae, but how could she help me? I had yet to heed the advice she had already given me: to tell Stas about the way things were with Jack. I thought of calling my sister, but *Payback* wasn't something I could talk about with her.

In bed that night beside Stas, I could not get warm. Panic

lodged in my throat, made it hard to draw a deep breath. I clutched at him with icy fingertips, pressed my feet against his legs.

"Leda, do you feel all right?" he asked.

"Stas, hold me," I whispered.

His arms encircled me in the dark.

"Is something the matter?"

"I think I might be getting sick," I said. My teeth were chattering.

"Poor little girl."

Within another minute, he was asleep again.

The next morning I woke to a heavy thud, as if something had been dropped on the floor downstairs. I sat up with the blanket held to my chest, eyes wide, heart pounding.

I was alone in the house. Stas had brought Clara to preschool on his way to work; they were long gone.

A minute went by, maybe two, and I heard nothing else. I wondered if I had dreamed it. I wondered too if the situation with Jack weren't making me a little crazy.

Just as I lay back down, a definite clattering. Like an object made of flimsy metal striking wood. And then the unmistakable sound of footsteps: a man's, heavy and deliberate. Coming from below, from inside the house.

Even in the midst of my fear, which flooded my mouth with a metallic tang, it occurred to me that whoever was downstairs was making no effort to be stealthy. Maybe Stas had forgotten something and come back for it.

It felt especially compromising to be in bed. Clad only in underwear and a long t-shirt, with bare legs and no bra.

In the bottom drawer of the night table beside the bed was Stas' handgun. Soon after Clara was born, he'd taken me to a shooting range and showed me how to use it. Even at the time, I knew I wouldn't be able to do it under duress. The chamber was hard to manipulate and just loading it had frightened me. If Clara were here, if she were in the house and her safety was at stake, I might manage it. As it was, I never even considered taking it out of the drawer.

But where was my cell phone? For maybe the twentieth time, I regretted that we had no land line and that I didn't make a point of keeping my cell by the bed. Right now it was in my purse, which was in the kitchen. Twitching with fear, I eased out of bed and reached for the nearest clothes, those at the top of the laundry basket. Stas' plaid boxers, which served as a flimsy pair of shorts. A Guatemalan sweater of rough red and orange wool, which I pulled on over my t-shirt; this wasn't the time to fumble with a bra. My heart was hammering, my breath coming in shallow little gasps.

And now, from the ground level of the house, came the sound of our portable radio, tuned to a country station. Would a rapist or burglar turn on the radio? I made myself peer around the door of my bedroom, where I could see down the steps and into the kitchen. My purse was on the kitchen counter, just where I'd left it the night before. Would a robber leave a purse untouched? There was a clear path to the door; no one was in sight. I could dash down the stairs and out to the street. Barefoot and shivering, a strange sight in the bright sweater and oversized plaid boxers, but safe from harm in any case—safe from whoever had invaded the house.

Yes. That was what I would do.

And then, without warning, Jack strolled into view and I screamed.

"Oh, hey! Oh hey, oh man, I'm sorry," he said, backing away and holding up both hands as if to show he wasn't armed. "I didn't know you were here. I left a note on the door saying I was inside."

I stood there staring at him and trying to get my breath back.

"I need to go to Yakima tonight on an emergency," he continued. "And I couldn't see leaving you guys hanging in the middle of the job, with a half-painted room. I just thought I'd get in here, get it done. I didn't think you'd mind. I never meant to surprise you or scare you. Like I said, there's a note right on your front door."

Finally I found my voice. "How did you get in?" I asked faintly.

"I got a key. I've had it so long I never even thought to mention it. Forgot I even had it, to tell the truth. I just remembered this morning because I was wishing I could get in here and then it came to me that I *could* get in. Walt gave it to me back in the day. Here, take it." He reached in his pocket, pulled out a mass of keys, and began working one of them loose. "Look, I'm real sorry. I wish I'd waited. I just wanted to do the right thing." He slid a key off its ring and held it out. "Here you go."

I took it wordlessly before turning away. Back in the bedroom, I quietly locked the door behind me. Then I stood in the middle of the floor, clutching the key, and started to cry. I was still crying half an hour later as I called my husband on his cell. "There are things I haven't told you," I said, and then I told him everything.

"Listen to what I say. I will be there in twenty minutes. I want you to go out to that car they gave you, and sit in it until I come home. Just stay there on the street in front of the house and make sure he does not steal anything. When you see that I have arrived, I want you to drive away. All right?"

"Where am I supposed to go?"

"Go any place you want."

"What will you do?"

"I am going to put a stop to this."

"How?"

"Do not worry about this," Stas told me. "It is not any longer your concern. And do not speak about this to anyone."

"But Stas—"

He hung up.

I went out without a word to Jack and got into the Pontiac. As Stas had ordered, I sat there waiting. The morning was very warm.

I understood that whatever happened next, nothing would be the same. This phase of the game was over; no more pretense of neighborly ease would be required.

It was very hot in the Pontiac, but I kept the engine off, the windows up. People passed the car: skateboarders, dog-walkers, women with strollers. It occurred to me that anyone who noticed me might wonder why I was sitting there. No one could know that the house I was watching was my own. During the brief time we'd been here, I'd met none of our neighbors.

After about twenty minutes, my husband's black Civic appeared in my rearview mirror. He was at the wheel and beside him was a man it took a moment for me to place. It was the man from the warehouse, the one who had cut the stone for Stas that day. The scar running the length of his face made him unmistakable. I hadn't known they were in touch; Stas had not mentioned him since. He had short silver hair, a hard face, narrowed eyes. I had the impression that he was someone who seemed older than he truly was. That he might be in his late thirties while looking forty-five or even fifty: Russian men tended to age hard. Why was he here? To stand next to Stas and look intimidating? If that was the case, and I hoped it was, he would surely be very effective.

Both men nodded to me as they climbed out of the car but neither of them came over. It was as if I were incidental to whatever was about to happen. The man from the warehouse put on a pair of shades. As they walked together toward the house, I put the key into the ignition, shifted into drive, and pulled into the street. *It's done*, I thought then, and though I wasn't sure just what these words might mean, they seemed weighted with finality and portent and peril. I drove away.

11

There are things I haven't told you. That was my opening line upon calling Stas earlier. And then I recounted Jack's relentless overtures, his insinuation, his aggression. Even now, I wondered if I'd blown the whole thing out of proportion.

Who was the man with the scar? Was he part of the Russian mob? And what was Stas doing with him?

In a North Portland diner known for its blue cornmeal pancakes, I sat next to a window with a cup of decaf and stared at the white cherry tree across the street. By now, any confrontation in our home was likely over. Had Stas and the other man merely threatened Jack? Or could they possibly have hurt him?

Sitting there, a memory came to me, of the day that an angry ex-employee named Fred came looking for Stas. Fred was the initial answer to Bryce's ongoing conundrum: what meticulous, reliable person could stand to build the same computer hundreds or even thousands of times, forty to sixty hours a week, in a windowless room for minimum wage?

"I need Rain Man," he said. "No, seriously. And I think I found him. I talked to him on the phone this morning and I'm telling you he's the one." He slipped into a rendition of Fred's high robotic whine:

I built boxes for Compaq for five years and Hewlett Packard for eight years and Sony for six years and Dell for three years. I have my own T15 reversible torque screwdriver—

(Here Bryce had interrupted him to say, "If you're rocking back and forth right now, you're hired.")

But while Fred did indeed prove to be fastidious and tireless, Stas couldn't stand him. The ancient transistor radio he kept on his desk (despite Bryce's offer to buy him a Walkman or iPod) was always on, always tuned to an opera station. He had overwhelming body odor, was always muttering under his breath and often burst into high-pitched laughter for no reason. Michiko, Stas' most valuable employee, was afraid of him. For that matter, no one ever wanted to be alone with him.

After two months of this, Stas went to Bryce with the idea of outsourcing Kaiser Tech's computer assembly. He had compiled a list of vendors offering this service and Bryce had no trouble deciding on a fly-by-night operation favoring gray market parts and illegal immigrant labor at very competitive rates.

Three days after Stas fired him, Fred returned to the office. I was in the room when he appeared in his dirty trench coat. Stas was on the phone and he swiveled to face his former worker but did not hang up. Everyone stared as Fred lumbered over to Stas and unsheathed a blade from his pocketknife.

"Very good, Linda," Stas said into the receiver. "I will be in touch with you next week. In the meantime, do not hesitate to let me know if I can help in any other way."

Only after several more pleasantries did he replace the phone in its cradle. Then he stood with no apparent hurry or alarm.

"Hello, Stas," Fred said. He held the pocketknife in a loose grip and jiggled it as he spoke.

"Hello, Fred." Stas' voice was matter-of-fact, his gaze direct and perhaps a little pitying.

"How's it going, Stas?"

"Everything is all right, Fred. How are things going for you?"

Everyone else in the room was unmoving, eyes darting back and forth between the two men.

"How about your boxes, Stas? How are the factory boxes coming along?"

"They are fine, Fred. Why do you ask?"

And so it went, back and forth. Stas kept an even tone and continued to respond as if Fred were making friendly conversation. After a few more exchanges of this kind, Fred abruptly wheeled around and walked out.

Bryce was the first to speak. "Jesus Christ," he said. "We should call the police."

It occurred to me then that he hadn't moved to intervene or protect Stas in any way.

"Do not bother," Stas said. "He will not be back."

Remembering this now, I wondered again why Stas had not been afraid. Was it his own knife, the one he carried in his left boot? Was it just his ability to read people? And how had he honed that instinct? All he ever said in explanation was: "I knew that Fred would do nothing in the end."

When I came home, no one ambushed me on the driveway or tried to trail me into the house. There was no one inside the house either. Two of the walls in the nursery-in-progress were pale yellow and two remained a grayish-white. No traces of Jack were left in the room.

The silence and stillness felt like a benediction. I raised the blinds and the afternoon sunlight slanted in.

Stas did not answer his phone for the rest of the day and he did not return home until late that evening. When he came in, Clara was already asleep and I was waiting for him at the kitchen table.

"Stas," I said, as soon as his jacket was off. "Where have you been?"

He took the seat across from me. "Listen," he said. "This morning you said there was something you had not told me. Well, as it happens, there is something I have not told you in return."

I looked at him, waiting.

"The man who accompanied me earlier," he said. "His name is Vladimir."

"He's the one who trimmed our marble countertop."

"Yes. That is correct. And Vladimir is running his own business here in Vancouver. He is a contractor and he supplies building materials. Many of his clients are Russian."

"All right, and…?"

"He has offered me occasional work as he needs me. With deliveries, shipments, things of that nature. I am of use to him not only because I have done work of this kind before, but because I can speak English and Russian with equal proficiency. It is not hard to find Russian workers, but it is not so easy to find Russian workers with wonderful English." He smiled. "It will be no more than once or twice a month."

"But you already have a full-time job."

"I can make twice as much in a day with Vladimir as I can at Intel, and he pays me in cash besides. Therefore, when he needs me, I will arrange to take the day off. I will use a sick day or vacation day. So: as it happens, he asked me to assist him today."

He went on to say they'd gone to Yacolt for a limestone shipment, a drive of several hours each way.

"When did he ask you along?" I wanted to know. "How far in advance?"

"He told me about this job on Monday."

"Why didn't you mention it to me?"

"Well," said Stas. "I thought you might not like it if I use my vacation days in this way."

"Didn't you think I'd find out? Like the next time I try to plan a trip and you have no more time coming to you?"

"You see?" said Stas. "This is what I thought you would say. Yes, of course I knew that in time you would find out. But do you remember what Bryce used to tell us? 'It is better to ask forgiveness than permission.' " He smiled again, then added: "I thought you might not like it, but I also thought that right now it is necessary. We need the money, and—"

"Stas," I interrupted. "What happened this morning? With Jack?"

Stas paused, as if weighing what to say. "We had some words," he said at last.

When nothing more was forthcoming, I said, "Could you be a little more specific?"

"I told him, 'Look, we don't want you working on the house anymore. And do *not* talk to my wife anymore—if you have anything to say, you can say it to me.' Then I paid him for the first half of the job and that was it."

"And he left? Just like that?"

"Yes," Stas said.

"Well, but I mean, how did he react? He must have said *something*."

"He said, 'Okay.' "

"Just 'okay'? He didn't seem offended, or…or surprised…?"

"No," Stas said. "He did not seem surprised."

I sat there for a moment, taking this in.

"He said he understood," Stas added. "So is there anything to eat? I never had dinner."

I did not see Jack the next day, or the day after that. In fact, construction on the house next door seemed to be at a standstill; I saw no one there for days at a stretch.

Every morning I woke up happy, and it would take a moment to remember why. I no longer left the house with my eyes down and my shoulders drawn in; I no longer felt as if I were wandering into the sights of some surveillance instrument. I looked around at the sky, the birds on the telephone wire, the neighborhood kids on their scooters and skates. The construction van at the curb next door had lost its sinister aspect.

Back in the house again, I opened the curtains and even the windows, left the kitchen door ajar so the cat could come in and out. I hauled Clara's plastic play house from the garage to the front yard and hung the bird feeder from a tree within view of the living room. Patches of the lawn were turning brown and brittle from the recent drought, and now I dragged out the hose and watered the grass. The ache between my shoulder blades faded, then disappeared. My home had been returned to me.

That Friday morning, since there was no longer any reason not to have a cup of tea on the side porch, I was sitting there with the third-rate local newspaper when a car pulled to the curb next door. A lean man wearing a baseball cap got out and came around to our front walk.

"Leda," he called. As he drew closer, I saw that it was Walt.

"Walt," I said. "How's it going? We're still getting some of your mail, let me give it to you." I set my mug down and stepped into the house. Stas had stacked all of Walt's bills and letters and left them on the counter. I picked them up and returned to the front yard, where he stood squinting in the sunlight. "Can I get you some water or coffee or anything?"

"Oh, no, that's all right. But thank you. Hey, the place is looking good. Are you all settled in?"

"Getting there, I'd like to think. We really love the house."

"That's nice to hear." He hesitated. "I'm not sure how to put this. Well, let me just ask you. I'm wondering if you've seen Jack lately."

"Jack?"

"I haven't heard from him in a while. I know he was friendly

with you guys, did a little work for you, and I was just wondering if you've seen him around."

"Not since last week," I told him.

"Did he say anything to you about leaving town?"

"He said he was going to Yakima."

"That's where his wife lives. He was supposed to spend the
weekend with her but he never showed up. He hasn't answered
his cell since Friday or returned any of my calls. His boss said
he hasn't shown up for work either. I just don't know what to
think."

And what did *I* think, in that moment? I had no real foreboding yet. I thought that maybe Stas, or more likely Vladimir,
had scared Jack into blowing town. And if that was so, he'd left
his boss hanging. A boss he owed money, no less. It would
make sense for him to lay low for a while, in light of all that.

Still, when my husband came home, I told him, "Walt was
over here today."

"He was?" Stas said. "What did he want—his mail?"

"He wanted to know if we'd seen Jack."

Stas looked up from the stack of bills in front of him. "Jack?"

"Apparently, no one's seen or heard from him in days." I
watched his face as I said this. It didn't change.

"What did you tell him?"

"I said we hadn't seen him either."

"You did not mention anything about Friday?"

"Of course not."

"Well, good," Stas said. "He has no need to know about that."

12

That night in bed, as my husband slept, I found myself staring at the gold chain around his neck. Stas knew I didn't like it but he never took it off. It belonged to his best friend in Russia, a young man named Alexei who—upon going to prison—had given it to Stas for safekeeping. My husband wrote to Alexei every month, and once or twice a year he received a letter back: a few terse lines in Cyrillic asking about Stas' family, sending his regards, never saying a word about himself or his situation. Stas never expected to see him again.

"What was his crime?" I asked early on.

"He was involved with the wrong people."

"Okay, but what did he do?"

"He was convicted of robbery and assault."

"Nice friend to have."

"I said he was convicted of these. I did not say he was guilty. My guess is that it was a set-up."

According to Stas, the Russian police were criminals themselves: all of them. "You think American police are corrupt?" he would say. "You have no idea what corruption is."

"Stas, tell me—were *you* mixed up in anything bad there?"

"Not really."

"What does that mean—*not really*?"

"It means no."

Stas had never been back to Russia. He claimed that he would be arrested if he ever did go back.

"Arrested for what?"

"For draft evasion. For my refusal to rape and murder the Chechens."

I had to wonder, now, whether this was the real reason.

"What if your mother were dying?"

"I could not go and see her."

How did it feel to break with everyone you'd ever known and everything you'd been? Because Stas did not have much to say about this, his few words on the subject had been memorable.

"Before I met you," he told me once, "I had no feelings left. I was nothing but a cold heartless surviving machine."

It pleased me to hear this, of course. It pleased me to think I'd restored and redeemed him. I'd never really thought about the cold or heartless part.

Tonight we had gone to bed early. Stas fell asleep within minutes while I lay awake and brooded about him. Now it was almost two in the morning. In all this time, he had barely stirred.

"Are you Mrs. Vasiliev?"

The man on the side porch was about five-foot-seven and somewhat heavyset, with dark hair shorn to within a quarter inch and small, close-set eyes. His face was flushed from the heat and his collar stained with sweat. He had the labored breathing of a smoker and his clothes, too, bore the scent of cigarettes.

"Yes," I said, after a startled pause. I hadn't expected a stranger to know who I was, and even after two years, I was still taken aback whenever I heard myself identified in this way. Not as Leda Reeve, or Ms. Reeve, but as some Russian man's wife.

He lifted one of his lapels to show me a badge, then withdrew a business card from an inner jacket pocket. "Mrs. Vasiliev, I'm Detective Rayburn. Your name was mentioned to me by

Walter Marcum, in connection with the disappearance of his cousin, Jack Shelby. We're trying to speak with anyone who might have seen him during his last days here in town." He passed me the card and I took it, shifting Clara to one hip while I stared at its spare black print.

"He's officially missing?" I said. "I knew Walt was having trouble getting hold of him, but I didn't realize it was anything serious."

"Do you have a few minutes right now, Mrs. Vasiliev?"

"I don't have to be anywhere until one," I told him. "Would you like to come in? Can I get you a cup of coffee?"

We sat at the kitchen table while Clara played with a set of stacking rings on the floor. "Pretty little girl you got there," he remarked.

"Thank you."

"So what can you tell me," he asked, taking out a notepad, "about your acquaintance with Mr. Shelby?"

"Well, let me see. I met him the day before we moved in," I said. "He was working next door. He introduced himself to me and told me he was Walt's cousin. And he was very helpful with some of our household issues—he was able to turn our water on, for one thing, and he fixed a leak in our ceiling. We knew he was hoping for paid work of some kind, and we eventually hired him to paint one of our rooms."

I was amazed by how steady and matter-of-fact I sounded, as if this were the role I'd been waiting for all my life. Meanwhile, I tried to imagine what the detective was seeing. I was grateful that Clara was wearing a little pink smock dress and that her face was clean and rosy-cheeked. I was glad, too, to be visibly pregnant, glad to be wearing my own modest dress with its gentle old-fashioned pattern of cornflower-blue roses. Surely this mother-and-child picture could arouse no suspicion.

Everything I noticed about the detective, on the other hand, seemed to confirm our advantage. His suit was cheap, and he had bad teeth, crooked and streaked with nicotine. His fingernails were ragged, as if he bit them.

"About how often would you say you talked with him?" he wanted to know next.

"Well, probably close to every day for a while. I mean, he was right next door, so he'd see me coming and going, and he seemed anxious to be helpful and neighborly. Like he knew my husband was concerned about a rodent problem in the garage, and he brought over a bunch of traps. Things like that."

What was agonizing was not being able to ask questions of my own. Questions like, *Why are you really here? Are you questioning me as a witness or a suspect? A suspected accomplice? Do you have anything on my husband?* Without knowing the context of this little chat, I couldn't know what details were safe to disclose.

For instance, should I tell the detective how thoroughly Jack had unnerved me? That could only invite closer scrutiny. But if I said nothing about that, and somehow it came to light, would it render my testimony suspicious?

"When was the last time you saw him?"

And here I felt the first pang of fear. I sat there as if trying to remember. Stas had said, *Do not speak of this to anyone.* But refusing to talk to the detective could come to no good, and it was too dangerous to make up details I might need to remember and defend.

"Last Friday morning."

"Morning of the eighth, okay. And where was this?"

"He came over to finish painting the room."

"Gotcha," he said, writing. "And what time was that, would you say?"

"Around nine-thirty in the morning."

"Very good. And when did he leave?"

I took a drink of coffee; it was some effort to swallow. "I'm not sure. I went out for a while and when I came back he was gone."

"You left him in the house while you were away?"

"Yes."

In the silence that followed, I felt compelled to add, "I wasn't worried about theft since he was working right next door."

"That makes sense," the detective said. "My wife and I would do the same. We figure if we know who you are and where to find you, well, you'd have to be pretty dumb to steal something, wouldn't you?"

Again I tried to read the man in front of me. Was he one of those deceptive types—comfortable, affable, the kind who lulled you into thinking they were befuddled and sweaty and clueless until the noose was around your neck? Or was he truly as he seemed—a fourth-rate dick detailed out here to the sticks, thinking mostly about the buttermilk biscuits in his lunchbox? I couldn't tell.

"What time did you return to the house?" he asked next.

"Around eleven."

"And Mr. Shelby was gone by that time."

"Yes, he was."

"Had he finished painting the room?"

"No," I said. "Not quite."

"How much progress had he made? I'd just like to determine when he might have left."

"Uh, not very much."

The detective paused in his note-taking and looked at me. "And yet he was gone when you came back. Did you wonder about that at all, or—?"

I made myself meet his gaze. "You know, he'd been in and out a lot. He seemed to be someone with a lot of drama in his life. He'd mentioned an emergency in Yakima, so I thought maybe he just cut out earlier than planned. And there's no real urgency yet with this paint job...I mean, we won't need a finished nursery for several more months." Here I put a hand on my swelling belly and attempted a maternal smile.

The detective hadn't taken his eyes off me. "I understand. Still, the guy comes over to finish the room, he leaves without doing anything much, and for the next week you don't see hide nor hair of him. If it was me, I would be aggravated. At the very least, I'd wonder."

His tone had changed. This was subtle but unmistakable. *He knows*, I thought. (Knows *what*?) It was essential, I told myself, not to seem defensive.

"When you put it that way, it does seem strange," I said. "I don't know why I didn't give it much thought. To tell you the truth, the man could be a little overbearing. He kind of took any opportunity to talk to me, and he talked a lot. Not seeing him for a few days was a little bit of a relief."

"Would you say you were on friendly terms, though?" the detective pressed. "Or was there maybe some bad blood brewing there?"

"No, we were friendly," I told him. "I mean, even when I was anxious to get away from him, I tried not to seem impatient."

"Were you happy with his work? So far, at least?"

"The paint job?" I said. "It was fine as far as I could tell. Do you want to see it?"

I regretted the question the moment I'd asked it. Even to myself, I sounded too eager. To accommodate, to seem helpful, to yield information and access—as long as it was useless. But if the detective saw it this way, he didn't show it. On the contrary, he actually followed me down the stairs to peer at the two yellow walls.

Before he left, he said he'd be back to talk with Stas.

13

"Leda. Tell me exactly. I need to know exactly what you said to this detective about last Friday."

"I already told you! Three or four times already! Stas, how many times do you need to hear it?"

"You did not mention me or Vladimir."

"No. I told you I didn't."

"Okay," Stas said. "Okay." He raked at his hair with both hands. I could see that he was afraid, and it was making me afraid.

We were speaking in hushed tones in the backyard because Stas thought the detective might have bugged the house. He had gotten down on his knees to look at the underside of the wooden kitchen table.

"Stas, you're freaking me out. What are you afraid of? You told me nothing happened with Jack, that you had some words, that was all."

"And this is true. But if something has happened to him, it is possible that they will try to pin it on me."

"What could have happened to him?"

"How can I know this? But it seems he is missing."

I felt my own eyes narrow as I stared at him. I was holding myself with crossed arms, to keep from trembling.

"Why was Vladimir with you that day?"

"He was with me because we were going to Yacolt."

"No, come on, Stas, don't play dumb. He got out of the car with you. He put on those shades like some thug in a movie."

"Yes. Exactly like in a movie. That is exactly why. He did this just for—how do you say?—for kicks. Because he knows the way he looks, with the scar. Like a gangster. He enjoys it."

For a moment, I let myself be reassured. But then Stas looked away and I had no idea what to believe.

Going back inside our home was like walking onstage after conferring urgently in the wings. Because of my husband's idea that the house might be wired, we kept our conversation not only free of references to Jack, but stilted in every way. We talked the way we might talk in public, aware that others were listening.

"Very good dinner, honey," Stas told me.

"I'm so glad you like it. Lillian sent me the recipe. I wouldn't have thought of putting olives and dates together in a marinade, but it's really nice, isn't it? Clara, sweetie, can you have another little bite of chicken?"

"Will it be this hot tomorrow, do you know?"

"I don't think the heat's going to break for a while."

"Would you please state your full name, slowly and clearly, for the record?" Detective Rayburn had exchanged his notepad for a tape recorder. It was Saturday and he was back, as promised, to talk to Stas.

"Stanislav Ivanovich Vasiliev," Stas said.

"Mr. Vasiliev, do you know why I'm here?"

"I understand that Jack Shelby is missing," Stas said carefully.

"Well, as a matter of fact, we have reason to believe he's dead," Rayburn said.

"*Dead?*" This came from me.

"Yes, ma'am." He was looking at me steadily, as if he knew how I felt at that moment. And how did I feel? Shocked and thrilled and sick and hollow.

"That's...that's awful," I said. "Are you sure?"

"Well, let's see. He's been married eleven years, and he's never gone a full week without contacting his wife. For that matter, his cell phone hasn't been used at all during the last seven days, and he hasn't used his ATM card either. He disappeared right before payday, leaving all of his possessions, including his truck and his dog. In our experience," he concluded, "factors like these usually point to the worst."

I turned to Stas, who looked pale and stricken. As I glanced back and forth between him and the detective, it came to me with sudden, unequivocal clarity: Stas did it. He killed Jack.

You hear these stories. You see them on the news or read them in women's magazines. Half the tabloid headlines, it would seem, have to do with elaborate deception and betrayal. *He led a double life*. At the heart of each of these stories: a long-married woman whose image of her husband has cracked open like an egg and hatched a snake. *Her world was shattered*.

But in fact, the most surreal aspect of situations like this is that your world is not shattered. The detective leaves and the house is still standing, the leaves are still drifting into the street in front of it, the same kids are clattering by on bicycles and skateboards. The only difference is within, the rising panic and disbelief, the weakness in your limbs. All the thoughts in your head have been replaced by a single question: *what should I do?* But perhaps the strangest, most staggering truth of all is there is no need to do anything. You can keep on just as before. Life inside your house has become theater and you need only adhere to your usual script.

It used to be a joke of mine. I used to joke that Stas was probably a spy or a gangster, working for the KGB or the Russian mafia, that his interest in weapons and body armor was likely not as innocent as he'd have me believe. That one day, after he'd committed some atrocity or terrorist attack, the F.B.I. would interrogate me and the media would expose me for my nearly unbelievable naiveté.

So, Mrs. Vasiliev (I'd drawl mockingly, with the southern inflection I associated with federal officers), *as your husband accumulated a stockpile of ammunition…and an arsenal of guns…and a closet full of Kevlar…did it ever! occur to you! that perhaps he was up to something less than wholesome?*

And then I'd provide my own imagined answer, in the voice of a half-wit. *Oh gee, no, officers, I never did think anything of it… I just figured it was a harmless little hobby…*

But when it happens, when you're truly forced to revise the meaning of the clues you've disregarded, there's no humor in it, only breathlessness and dread. My husband, the father of my little girl: a killer. Sleeping beside me every night for more than a thousand nights: a murderer. Not prowling in the shadows or watching through the window or lurking in the basement, but entwined with me, inside me, naked and pressed up against me. If you're lucky, you can rid yourself of the wolf at your door, but what do you do when the wolf is in your bed?

You think: *I have to tell someone about this or go out of my mind.* But who can you tell? It's not a conversation you can have on the phone. Nothing you can discuss over coffee or cocktails. Not something you can disclose even to your friends or family.

I thought: *Stas and I need to talk about this.* But this thought was replaced almost immediately by: *he can't ever suspect that I know.*

Sometimes I wavered, retreated from my own conviction. Impossible. Impossible that he could have killed Jack: it was broad daylight. He would have to have done it in a way that left no blood, which would rule out the use of his guns or knives.

And then he'd need to get rid of the body. How would he know how to do something like that? But what did I know about what Stas knew?

And Jack was dead; the detective was sure of that.

Maybe Stas had been mixed up with the mob before coming to America; maybe that was why he couldn't go back. Maybe that was how he knew the friend who was in prison. Maybe he'd had terrorist training.

Were those hands going to close around my throat one night? Could his love for me be nothing but an elaborate and long-term pretense? If it was, he was far better at acting than I'd ever been.

In all the bewilderment, the vertigo, the upended perspective of a funhouse mirror, one lone conviction was still in place: Stas loved Clara. Nothing in the world could make me doubt that. He had spent countless hours bathing her, playing with her, stretched out asleep on the floor beside her crib when she couldn't bear to be left alone in the room. I knew at least that he would never hurt her, and it followed that—if only for her sake—he would not hurt me either. For this reason alone, my life was unlikely to be in danger.

There are no words for the shock. Of finding yourself in this place, this far-flung edge of your own life. Weighing the possibility that your husband might kill you. Alone in the world after all.

That night in bed, Stas put a hand over my mouth as he had done so many times before, his thumb grazing my lips. He did not speak. My skin tingled as I imagined him closing off my breath. Something I asked of him early and often was to hold my wrists above my head, look straight into my eyes, and keep a flat impassive expression throughout the act of sex. The face of a card sharp, that was what I wanted: the face of an executioner. *Be careful what you wish for.*

Tonight he did this—it seemed to me, anyway—with a special deliberation, as if he could sense my fear of him and had no wish to dispel it. As he pressed into me, he closed one fist around my hair and flattened his other palm across my bared teeth, all while staring into my eyes with what could only be called a vengeance. And suddenly from within me came a white-hot answering flash, like oil flung into a hot pan or the silver of a hooked fish catching the sun. I bucked and twisted and thrashed and caterwauled; I screamed into his hand. This seemed to go on and on; I could not get enough. Even after my husband was spent, I lay there clutching his back with both hands, the motion of my hips convulsive, compulsive, thrusting against his of their own accord. I was whimpering.

Sex with Stas had always been more than satisfactory, but this was something else; this was a revelation.

Even after all motion had subsided, and we lay there in stillness, I continued to whimper: a whelp in her first heat.

Spokoyno, Stas whispered after a while. Then, by way of translation: *Shhhh.* I wondered whether anything would ever surprise me again. He had never spoken to me in Russian before.

On the night table, my cell phone began to vibrate and when I made no move to pick it up, the call went to voicemail. It was Rae, inviting me to lunch.

During the spring before any of this happened, when Rae and I had our conversation about intimacy, I said many different things about my decision to marry Stas, and all of them were true.

I said, "Before Stas, I'd never had a romantic relationship that began as a friendship. But Stas and I worked together, day in and day out, for over a year before we started dating. And by that time, I had already come to trust him."

I said, "I had no doubt that he would be a good husband and eventually a wonderful father."

I said, "I was able to choose a real partner because I was finally ready."

There were other things I didn't say.

I didn't say: *I was tired. I was tired and I didn't think I had it in me to go another round in the old ring.*

Or: *I probably needed to marry someone I didn't really know. Someone with so much built-in mystery that I might never really know him. I knew so little about him when I married him that it was almost like an arranged marriage. Except that I arranged it myself.*

I never said: *I'd begun to notice that my status as a single woman left me at a disadvantage in my relationships with married men. During fights, during holidays, and in the wake of every breakup, they went home to their wives and I went home alone. So a basic inequity was always there, a source of leverage I could never access. And at some point, I actually told myself: you know what, I'll get married too, and that will level the playing field for future trysts.*

These were things I didn't tell Rae, and all of them were true as well.

Having failed to disclose all this, I could hardly reveal the punch line: that something funny happened on the way to the altar. That I fell in love with my fiancé, came to see him as someone I would never betray.

The joke would have been on me if Stas himself were revealed, later, as the type to stray. But I'd never seen any such tendency in him. He was a hard-working, stoical, one-woman man, as far as I could tell.

There was a refrain I kept hearing from young women, when they were parting ways with some liar or cheat or deadbeat. I'd overhear them in coffeehouses and cafés: talking to their friends, or into their cell phones, or even to the men who had disappointed them. Over and over, I heard: *I deserve better*. Well, in my case, the opposite was true: surely I deserved worse.

14

"Angel called last night," Rae reported at Mona's, a café in downtown Vancouver. "He just got out of Red Rock and he wanted to come over. It took everything I had—and I do mean everything—not to let him."

"Red Rock?"

"Oh, sorry. That would be the Arizona state pen."

"What was he in for?"

"This time? He shot out someone's kneecaps. He would have been in longer, but half a dozen witnesses heard the other guy threaten Angel earlier that night. Plus the guy can still walk. He needs a cane, but at least he's not in a wheelchair or anything."

"Rae," I said. "Is there anything Angel could do that would change your feelings about him? I don't mean anything he could do to you—I mean something he might do to someone else."

"I don't know," she said. "I mean, I guess so—like if he hurt a little kid or something. But he would never do that. He's in the life, in the game, and there's a certain honor to it. He wouldn't hurt anybody who wasn't trying to hurt him or his people first."

"What if…" I said. "Just, as a hypothetical question—what if he killed someone?" I didn't quite manage to look at her as I asked this.

"To tell you the truth? He probably has," she said. "But no. That's not something that would change the way I feel about him."

"Rae. I know you have great sex with this guy," I said. "But aside from that. Do you really love him?"

"I really love him."

*

Something changed after this conversation. Had I just needed permission? To accept what Stas had done? After talking with Rae, something shifted, lifted, inside me. As I got into my car, I felt a certain lightness. I had wished Jack were dead, and now he was. I felt lithe and agile and devious. Glinting with secrets, with hidden power.

For the first time since the earliest days of our marriage, Stas and I had sex every night. All day, all evening, I waited for it. The moment Clara was asleep, I tugged him toward the bed. I would join him in the shower without warning, straddle him at his desk when he was working. When we weren't in bed, I would stare at him as I'd stared at Clara for the first few days after she was born. It was as if I were seeing him for the first time. During weekday afternoons, when Clara was napping, I lay in our bed and touched myself, thinking only of him.

Every day I recorded more poems and often they took on a special resonance.

> *Now I'll take to bed*
> *this body and the phantom*
> *of what it once was, inseparable*
> *as they are these days, smoke*
> *rising from a stubborn fire.*

In an upscale maternity boutique in Portland, I bought a sassy bikini set: a black bra with a pink satin bow front and center; a matching g-string with its bow at the back.

"What is this about a movie you were in?" Stas asked me one night. "What is the name? *Back Pay?*" This actually made me laugh now.

"*Payback.*"

"It was a porn movie?"

"Not hard-core porn. And I didn't have real sex with anyone

but my boyfriend," I said. "But beyond that, there was plenty of nudity and simulation. I mean, it was trashy."

"Did you need money at that time?" Stas asked. "What made you decide to be in a movie like this?"

"I wanted to," I said. "I was nineteen."

And although we had just made love, I felt him harden once more against the round swell of my belly.

The days grew longer. In late June, I felt the baby move for the first time. Not long after that, we went for an ultrasound and were jubilant to learn I was carrying a boy. We decided to make the nursery walls Wedgwood blue instead of yellow. Stas declared he would do it himself and made good on his word the very next weekend.

We spent the Fourth of July holiday in Seattle, visiting some old friends, leaving late in the afternoon the Thursday before. It was the first road trip I could remember where Stas and I didn't argue. I let him play Frank Sinatra all the way there. He let me plan too many activities. We went to Pike Place market for *piroshkis*; we took Clara to the aquarium. On Friday evening, the Fourth, we rode a ferry to Bainbridge Island, just Stas and me—Clara was asleep at the house of our hosts. From a blanket on the waterfront beach, we watched the fireworks over Eagle Harbor.

Lying there with my husband's arm around me, my head on his shoulder, the fireworks bursting against the black sky, it came to me that I was happier than I had ever been. And yet this happiness didn't feel the way I'd always imagined it would. It felt fearful and precarious. As if it might be taken from me at any moment.

I hadn't really considered our situation until now, hadn't let myself consider it. Being here in Seattle allowed me to look at it sidelong; it was the distance between us and the detective. We hadn't seen him during the last week or two, but I knew his work on Jack's case was far from over. He was investigating a murder. It didn't get more serious than that. He wasn't going to just give up and go away for good. He would be back and likely it was just a matter of time before something tipped him off to Stas' involvement. Wasn't that the way it always happened? In books and in movies, the killer always made some slight and yet fatal mistake.

If Stas was caught—oh, it made my throat tight just to think about it—if he were caught, then he would be taken away from me for decades, maybe even forever. And just like that, overnight, I'd be a single mother with an infant and a toddler. I'd be alone with the two of them twenty-fours a day, seven days a week—at least for the next several years, until they were old enough for school.

But no. No, of course it wouldn't be like that. As staggering a thought as that was, it was sheer wishful thinking next to the certain reality that I'd have to go back to work, and Clara and her brother would be in some cheap wretched day care unless the rest of my family was willing to treat me as a perpetual charity case.

And Stas. Stas would be locked away. In some terrifying, hard-core facility for violent inmates. I tried to imagine visiting him in such a place. Hauling the kids on some unspeakable hours-long car trip every few weekends to the hellhole where their father was caged. I imagined the humiliation, the isolation, of having a husband behind bars. And not for corporate fraud, or embezzlement, or writing bad checks, but for murder. I would no longer be seen as having married an enterprising, bootstrapping, self-made young man. He'd be just another Russian thug.

I started to hyperventilate and had to sit up. In a moment, I felt Stas' hand on my shoulder.

"What is it, Leda?"

"I just—oh God—I just felt so nauseous all of a sudden."

Stas accepted this, as I knew he would. I was pregnant, after all. I made myself slow my breathing and after a moment, I lay back down.

What if we went on the lam? Now, before Stas was even wanted by the law? We were so near the Canadian border. We could cross it and just keep going. And then what? If we were a young and childless couple, we could do anything. We could be migrant workers on a farm or deck hands on a ship. We could go wherever the wind took us, wend our way through Europe, reinvent our lives. We could start over, as Stas seemed so adept at doing.

But none of this could be done with a one-year-old in tow and a baby on the way.

Maybe Stas could strike out on his own, set himself up somewhere and send for us later. He wouldn't need an I.D. to buy an Amtrak ticket. He could cross the country by train, disappear into Brighton Beach, give up his hard-won English and his hopes for American citizenship. He could get the kind of job offered by men like Vladimir: off the books and paying in cash.

We could join him later—a year or so later, maybe. In the meantime, I'd tell the detective Stas had left me and I didn't know where he was. I'd give birth in a hospital while I still had health insurance. I would drain my bank account slowly, put the money in a suitcase. Sell the house, though breaking even was probably my best hope. Sell our cars, sell everything we owned. I pictured a yard sale with all our possessions on the lawn. I imagined a sign that said, *Everything Must Go*.

How would we cross the country without leaving a trail? Not by plane and not in a car. Like Stas before us, we could pay cash for train tickets, travel east over the course of several days. I pictured our family reunion in some cramped apartment above a Russian storefront.

These scenarios were all unthinkable; they were all impossible. All I wanted was what we already had. A house with a yard, a swing on a tree, a leafy front walk where one day I'd wait with my children for a school bus. There was nothing I wouldn't give—nothing at all—just to keep everything the way it was.

We returned late Sunday night, well after dark, and as I got out of the car, I nearly wept at the sight of our damp lawn, the sound of crickets, the bright stars above and the fragrance of woodsmoke. Would it ever feel safe to savor these things, or would I always be waiting for that knock at the door, the slow whirl of red and blue lights in our driveway, the flash of a badge that would level our lives?

It was the very next morning that I saw the article. A newspaper—the local one, *The Columbian*—was spread open on a table at the neighborhood bagel place. On the lower section of the front page were two photographs side by side.

One of them was Jack. I felt the recognition in my body—a stab of the old fear—before I'd even named him to myself. It took another moment to identify the second photo as that of the boss next door.

CONSTRUCTION OWNER CONFESSES TO MURDER OF MISSING VANCOUVER MAN read the headline.

Warren Albertson, detained Friday night as a suspect in the murder of Jack Shelby, confessed to the crime Saturday afternoon, investigators reported. Albertson, 44, told police that he bludgeoned his longtime employee with a crowbar before choking him to death, then buried his body beneath the house they were renovating. Jack Shelby's remains were unearthed by sheriff's investigators following the confession. Clark County coroner Dr. Gavin Blackwell confirmed multiple signs of blunt force trauma to the face and skull. He also cited injury to the neck consistent with manual strangulation.

I eased myself into the nearest chair and sat there, clutching the newspaper in both hands and staring at Warren Albertson's grainy little mug shot. The suddenness of it left me blindsided.

This man had killed Jack. Not Stas.

Not Stas.

I stayed at the table for several minutes, trying to take in this information. It was a long time before I was able to lay the paper aside. How many days had I been walking around with the conviction that Stas had done it? I hadn't realized how much space this belief had occupied until it was suddenly dismantled. What amazed me was how hard it was to let go of the idea—the idea of Stas as the killer. Maybe it was even harder to dispel than it once had been to absorb.

I went out to the parking lot with the newspaper and got into my car, where I sat behind the wheel and stared through the windshield.

There was relief, yes. The relief of surfacing from the dangers in a dream, to find yourself not only safe but restored to the familiar contours of your life: the solidity of your body, your bed. All the circumstances you checked at the threshold of sleep.

Relieved and restored and unburdened and bereft.

I wanted to tell someone, but there was no one to tell. Nobody knew I'd suspected Stas in the first place.

"I saw the paper and couldn't believe it," Rae told me over the phone. "That was your guy, right? The stalker next door? Maybe it was wrong to feel this way, but God help me, I said good riddance! I said, what a great break for Leda. And a great break for me too, because now I don't have to get Angel to rub him out! Ha ha, just kidding, of course."

"I couldn't believe it, either," I said. "Though I can't say I was too sorry to learn of it."

"Oh, honey, you must be so relieved. I know I would be. Don't feel bad about that—after what he put you through, anyone would feel that way."

When my husband came home, I showed him the clipping. He closed his eyes and exhaled sharply and I saw how afraid he had remained until now. Just before we sat down to dinner, Stas opened a bottle of wine and afterward he spent almost an hour playing with Clara. But later, when we got into bed, I pulled away when he reached for me. For the first time in more than three straight weeks, I told him I was tired.

"That is all right, honey," he told me. I could tell he was disappointed, but at the moment it was hard to care.

I was disappointed too.

There was no longer a wolf at the door, no longer a wolf in my bed. That left only the wolf in my head.

More than an hour after Stas had fallen asleep, unable to sleep myself, I lay there and looked at the clean lines of his back, the glint of the gold chain around his neck, the plaid of his flannel pajama pants.

A memory came to me: a spring night during our engagement. I was at an off-Broadway theater with my friend Cecily. We had arrived early because she was in a wheelchair and often needed extra time and space to get settled. This evening, the situation was especially dire: her chair wouldn't fit into the theater's narrow elevator and she had no other way to reach the seating area.

The manager was summoned and he was less than accommodating. The only way Cecily would be able to watch the show was if someone were to carry her to her seat, and he told us no staff person would be permitted to lift her. ("That would be a liability.") Nor would he allow us to seek help from any of the audience members filing in.

In desperation, I called Stas, who was dining with his former roommate in a restaurant across town. More than anything else he'd ever said or done up to that moment, I loved him for standing up midway through dinner, tossing money onto the table, apologizing to Dmitri, and taking a taxi across Central Park to lift Cecily from her wheelchair and carry her to her seat.

Lying there, staring at his back, I thought about his kindness during my pregnancy with Clara. How he wouldn't let me lift a thing, not even a grocery bag. I remembered my water breaking on my due date, an hour before midnight, the moment after I got into bed thinking, *Oh, well, not today after all.* In a private room at the hospital a couple of hours later, in the middle of the night, he slow-danced with me to the radio while the contractions were still mild.

A difficult time had followed the birth. Stas' first response to fatherhood was not elation or wonder or an excess of tenderness, but an air of resignation in the face of yet another endurance test. He was dutiful but moody, distant, just this side of begrudging. He slept on the sofa downstairs so he wouldn't have to wake in response to Clara's cries, as I did several times a night. This went on until the day he was standing over her at the changing table and she turned her head and smiled at him. Nothing was ever the same after that, and Clara's first word was *daddy*.

Just this morning, sitting on his knee at the breakfast table, she had spat a mouthful of chewed-up Cheerios directly into his own cereal bowl. He watched this happen without any expression and continued eating as before.

I resolved to make love to him in the morning. To wake him up that way.

At close to one A.M., I gave up on sleep and went down to the kitchen. I had decided to record the final poem in the book. The title was *A Postmortem Guide* and the dedication read:

For my eulogist, in advance. The narrator of the poem was leaving instructions for his own funeral speech.

Do not praise me for my exceptional serenity, it began.
Can't you see I've turned away
from the large excitements,
and have accepted all the troubles?

Go down to the old cemetery; you'll see
there's nothing definitive to be said.

Would Jack have a eulogy? Someone to say that despite a tough beginning in life, he'd been a hard worker, talented at construction, faithful in his fashion, kind to his dog?

And, please, resist the temptation
of speaking about virtue.
The seldom-tempted are too fond
of that word, the small-
spirited, the unburdened.

After our conversation that afternoon, Rae had sent me two text messages. She never wrote his name, but I knew they were about Angel. "I'm so weak! He showed up without warning and I let him in. Damn, damn, damn! I can't tell you how I hate myself!"

The second one, sent moments later: "P.S. It was fantastic."

Adam's my man and Eve's not to blame.
He bit in; it made no sense to stop.

Still, for accuracy's sake you might say
I often stopped,
that I rarely went as far as I dreamed.

With the construction boss in custody of the state, who would finish the house next door? And given its grisly history, who would ever move into it?

In a circle of lamplight in the darkened kitchen, I read the poem's ending into the recorder:

You who are one of them, say that I loved
my companions most of all.
In all sincerity, say that they provided
a better way to be alone.

PART TWO

Abel's Cane

I

Whenever the door to the office opened, Nan would listen for the bang of Abel's cane, striking one side of the entrance and then the other: a sound more soothing to her than rain on the roof. Sometimes he spoke to her as he passed the reception desk; sometimes he went by without a word.

She knew she should speak first. Otherwise he couldn't be sure she was there. More than once, she had come back from an errand or break to see him standing there, talking to the air.

But in his presence she was often overcome, and as often as not she said nothing when he came in, just stayed still and quiet and diffident and diligent and exultant.

Nan had met Abel when she interviewed for a job as his reader. There was no end to the printed material he needed to hear: leases, legal briefs, faxes, contracts, a few different newspapers and his daily mail. She was trying to figure out what, if anything, she could do in the real world, when she saw his want ad in the *Brooklyn Eagle*.

The interview took place at his home in Prospect Heights. It was a December morning and there was snow on the ground. For long minutes before their appointed meeting time, Nan stood on the sidewalk in front of his brownstone and felt afraid.

What was this fear about? She had never known anyone who was blind. Being alone with a blind man in his own house—he'd mentioned that his family was away for the weekend—was a strange and unsettling idea. But it was more than that. It had also occurred to her that much of what she usually relied on in a job interview would not help her in this one. Her dark blonde hair, pulled back into an elegant twist and pinned in place with lacquered chopsticks. The cut of her charcoal skirt and freshly ironed blouse; the dark stockings that hid the marks on the back of her legs; the mirror finish on her patent leather pumps.

It was disconcerting to realize how much she relied on her youth and beauty. But it went beyond that. There was also her array of appealing expressions—wide-eyed, impressed, sympathetic, sincere—that rarely failed to ingratiate her with others. In a job interview, she always looked straight into the employer's eyes and never let her gaze waver. On the other side of this man's threshold, with so much stripped away, Nan suddenly had no idea who she would even be.

Finally she went up his front walk, made herself ring the doorbell, and stood looking through one of the windows that flanked the door. His dog—a German shepherd with the weathered beauty of a wolf—appeared first, barking and showing teeth. Then the man himself materialized at the far end of the room, and through the warped and slightly darkened pane of what might as well have been one-way glass, she watched him grope his way toward her.

One of Abel's eyes was a prosthetic; the other was wandering and bleary. Both were pressed deep beneath the ridge of his jutting forehead. The sides of his head were dented in, as if mauled by forceps while the skull was still soft. His hair was a light brown gone halfway to gray, somewhat sparse in front and visibly brittle.

"Nan?"

"Yes," she said.

"I'm Abel."

His voice was a surprise. She had never spoken with him, only with his secretary, who managed his schedule and had set up this interview. With his first words to her, a certain understated yet unequivocal authority asserted itself so matter-of-factly that it was like being buoyed by a wave—a bodily and unreasoning happiness breaking over her before she knew why. He spoke with a self-assurance that bordered on indifference. His tone sought nothing—not attention nor approval nor agreement nor goodwill.

Nan clasped the hand he held out to her and looked around the front room, which was furnished in warm colors: wine and bronze and mahogany. There were oriental rugs and hanging tapestries and polished wooden furniture. When the dog darted behind her, she glanced over her shoulder and what she saw in the tarnished mirror above the fireplace stopped her breath. Up and down the back of her blouse were faint parallel lines of blood. The welts: she hadn't considered them at all, hadn't covered them with gauze or thought to wear a camisole…

It was a long and harrowing moment before she remembered that this particular interview would not be compromised by the oversight.

Abel said, "I was hoping to be able to speak with you right away, but something's come up and I need to make a phone call first. Why don't you go wait in my office—I shouldn't be too long."

He directed her to a set of stairs leading to the basement, and she went down to find a nearly empty room. After the lavish first floor, it looked especially spare, holding nothing but a battered desk, a couple of chairs, and a tired sofa against one wall.

Nan took a seat and waited. This seemed to be his domain within the house. The only thing to look at was a single framed photograph on his desk of a smiling woman with a little girl. There was nothing on the walls, no books or magazines, nothing to do but wait for him. But having heard his voice, the tension of waiting for him was not without some pleasure.

When after a full twenty minutes he appeared in the room, she asked, "Is this a picture of your wife and child?"

"That photo was taken more than a year ago," he said. "And Deirdre tells me that Lu looks very different already. But yes, it's the most recent one of the two of them that we've gotten around to framing."

"She—Lu?—she looks so different from the two of you." She looked in fact like she might have come from a former marriage. She had straight black hair, laughing black eyes, and a complexion the color of strong black tea. Whereas Deirdre, like Abel, was pale and light-eyed.

"Lulu was adopted," he told her.

He couldn't have known the effect these words would have on Nan. How could he have known? She wanted to tell him, "I was adopted too," but that would have been a half-truth at best.

As it was, she said nothing at all. Abel took the seat at his desk and asked, "Do you have a résumé?"

"Not with me," Nan said, alarmed. Because of course, she had no real résumé at all. "I didn't think I'd need one," she added.

"You don't, really," he said. "Not to be a reader. All that matters for this position is how you read. But I have a lot going on. Who knows what other uses I might find for you?"

And with this provocative choice of words, Nan liked to think that he started the game—the secret, sweet, and impossibly subtle game that sustained her for so long. And like all of their best moments, it was seamless. She heard his words, absorbed their little thrill, then spoke as if no underlying message had been sent or received.

She said: "I can bring one next time. Or I could get it to you within the next day or two."

"Well, let's see what happens," he decided. "Meanwhile, are you employed at this time?"

"I am. But I want to leave my job as soon as possible."

"Okay. And what are you doing now?"

There was a silence while Nan found herself in an unforeseen quandary.

"Hello?" he said after a long moment.

And then, instead of saying what she'd planned—that she was temping four or five times a week—Nan heard herself begin, falteringly, to tell him the truth. "I'm sorry," she said. "I'm not sure how to explain this. But the fact is that what I do is very strange."

"Oh?"

"Yes."

"Well, why don't you tell me what it is?"

It didn't seem possible to lie. She didn't feel like she had anything on him because she could see and he couldn't. She imagined that blindness had endowed him with a vast set of special powers: ears like a lynx, sonar like the bat, exquisite sensitivity, intuition bordering on clairvoyance. This turned out to be a romantic notion. People lied to him all the time. They had him sign doctored company checks, inflated the total on invoices and pocketed the difference, gave him one-dollar bills as change and told him they were other denominations. But for reasons having little to do with integrity, Nan never lied to him, then or ever.

"I work for a place called the Nutcracker Suite," she began.

"All right," he said, and waited.

"Have you heard of it?"

"I don't believe so."

"Well, then…do you know what a dominatrix is?"

"Yes," he said. "Is that what you are?"

"Well, in fact," she told him, "I'm the opposite. I'm a professional submissive."

She felt this information fill the space between them.

"Really?" he said at last.

"Yes."

She spoke quietly, without a hint of defiance or apology. She had to hope that her even tone would save her, because she knew that what she'd just confessed was worse than being a dominatrix. It was worse than being a stripper or even a whore. And the reasons for this went beyond the strange nature of the job—beyond, even, the idea that she might be mentally ill. More to the point was the fact that masochism was deeply unattractive. Nan understood this, because it repelled her too.

Abel did not respond with the questions other people always had. He didn't ask Nan what it was like, and so he didn't learn that men paid the house for an hour of her time in return for a menu of the ways they were allowed to punish her: a list of the implements at their disposal and others that could be wielded at extra cost. He didn't ask, either, why a poised, self-possessed and well-spoken young woman would let men hurt her for a living.

In fact, he asked no further questions at all about her current job, and she thought that under less desperate circumstances her confession would have ended the interview. But he was in dire need of a reader that day. His wife was out of town, he had no other interviews lined up for that afternoon, and the pile of papers on his desk was seven or eight inches high.

She imagined that he thought: *well, she's here, and I need someone now; I'll use her today, pay her and get rid of her, and next week I can find someone else.*

But then she began to read.

And she read as if this were an audition upon which her highest hopes were pinned. She read as if an oracle might be divined from the document if only it were rendered with enough care. She read with the reverence she'd once brought to her sessions at the Nutcracker, bending to the text like an animal to a river.

Within minutes it became clear that she could not possibly read too fast for Abel. (She learned later that he could absorb the contents of a cassette tape as it was being dubbed at high speed.) And she discovered also, only minutes into the venture, that reading like this—clearly, out loud, at an urgent pace for a long period of time—was not easy at all.

It was a task that demanded undivided attention—the discipline not to look up, for instance, when his dog ran into the room. It took a fierce and unrelenting focus to anticipate the inflection of a sentence before reaching the end of it; to scan ahead to upcoming words while forming the ones before; to articulate them precisely while rattling at the clip of an auctioneer. It took stamina to plow through page after page, and stoicism not to betray a flicker of fatigue. It took everything: back, shoulders, neck, eyes, lips, tongue, teeth, heart.

When Nan had read fifteen pages, he asked whether she was getting tired. She told him she wasn't. When she'd done thirty, he asked how much longer she could go on. I can go on as long as you want, she said. When she finished the first contract—a fifty-seven page document—he said, "You know, you're excellent. Really. Hands down, you're the best reader I've ever had."

"I'm so glad," Nan said.

"I'd love to keep going," he said. "But tell me—and please be honest—can you stand to read any more?"

"I would be happy to," she said, and it wasn't a lie. She couldn't say she wasn't suffering. But it was the kind of suffering she lived for—putting out, for all she was worth, for a man who would cherish the effort.

She read a second contract, thirty-four more pages of head-spinning legalese. After that, he said, "Okay. That was great. But by now, you must really want to get out of here."

"No," she told him. "I don't at all."

"You can say so, you know. If you reach a point where it's

making you crazy. It happens with most people. You can tell me and I'll understand."

"You'll never hear that from me," Nan said. Her voice shook just a little, saying this. "Please, I wish you wouldn't trouble yourself with that kind of concern."

If it were possible, she would have knelt before his chair and offered up this promise with both hands. But even as it was, there was an urgency to her words that he must have felt and understood. Because there was a certain acknowledgement in the pause that followed, before he said, "Okay."

Nan read to him for seven straight hours that day. Near the basement ceiling were high windows just at street level, and by four in the afternoon, the winter light was fading. Nearly every evening at this hour, a nameless sadness would threaten her with suffocation. But for once it felt as if the darkness closing in was nothing that could touch her. The wind was howling and the panes were frosted over and the room, suffused with a sienna light leaking in from the street lamp, felt like sanctuary.

In the convent, *sanctuary* referred to the chapel, but that was never an association Nan would have made herself. The chapel was a public and official space, with its stained-glass windows and deep red carpet, its icons and incense and velvet-draped altar. But just off the dais was a bare room where the sisters prayed away from public view. The rooms were connected by a single barred window, through which the priest dispensed communion. This room—where the sisters came several times a day for prayer, meditation, and petition—was her idea of sanctuary.

Everything Nan knew about the allure of servitude, she had learned from the sisters. The sun rose and set each day for nothing beyond the fulfillment of their wedding vows—poverty, chastity and obedience—a trinity in itself, of deprivation and self-denial and submission. Each nun bent her neck beneath that yoke and carried it without complaint. Slavery made them graceful, light on their feet beneath that floor-length cloth, floating like dark swans in their bridal black. They slept in stone cells with the doors ajar, fearing no evil and forgoing privacy. These cells were as bare as any in a prison, and there was nothing to set one apart from another. They spent hours on their knees—in prayer, at confession, on rice (a penance favored by Mother Immaculata), scrubbing floors—and the better part of every day was given to strict silence. Alone on their hard straw mattresses, they refrained from doing anything that would bring sexual release; their bodies had been given over, in their possession and yet no longer their own.

Nan thought that if the nuns could see her now, here with Abel, they would not disapprove. *Insofar as you did it for the least of my brethren, you did it for me*, Christ said, and she had always taken that to heart. Christ was truly in everyone, though many people made that difficult to believe. Abel made it easy, soft-spoken as he was: composed and self-contained, measured and resolute, with his low voice and light brown hair, his eyes the blue of a shadow on the snow.

Already she was longing to take that misshapen face in her hands, brush her lips over the afflicted lids, press her palms into the hollows at either side of his head. She used to dream of being touched in this way herself, of having someone fill in what was concave—but she no longer aspired to be milk-fed, sated. Better to be lean; better to be honed and lonely. She was worth more this way, to people like him.

"I can't believe this," Abel said, at around six o'clock in the evening. "I can't believe how much we've gotten done. I'm almost where I need to be. But I've got a meeting in another hour, so I need to wrap this up for tonight."

"All right," Nan said carefully. She felt weak with relief.

"Listen," he said. "I can't tell you how extraordinary this has been. And I know this is short notice, so I'll understand if it's not possible, but is there any chance you could come back tomorrow?"

"Just tell me what time."

That night she went back to the single room she lived in, a room not so different from Abel's basement, stripped off her blood-stained blouse and lay down on the narrow bed. She felt wrung out like a rag, as if she were emerging from a high fever: a dazed, languid, almost convalescent exhaustion, shot through with the warmth that always came to her in the wake of hard use. She was already more than half in love with him for exacting so much from her during what was supposed to have been an interview. He was a way out of what she was doing now; he was someone she could serve. And he wanted her early the next day.

She fell asleep within minutes, drugged by this reassurance, and in the morning she got up and did it all again.

And so in this way Nan became his reader, a job that filled about twelve hours a week. She read to him for a little over a month, an interval that seemed to assure him that she was reliable, tireless and apparently sane. So when a position as his full-time assistant opened up in his office—a job where she could answer the phone, manage his calendar, and read to him as well on a daily basis—he offered it to her and she leapt at it.

"You've been here four years," Mistress DeVille said when Nan gave the Nutcracker notice. "You really think you'll be able to stand a straight job?"

"I could if I had the right boss."

❀

Abel's office was at the edge of Bedford, about two miles from her rented room. She walked to work each weekday morning and back again in the evening, a ritual that began on the first day of her full-time employment. Everything looked different that morning: the snow dusting every surface, the trees glistening with ice, the sunrise glazing the dampened streets. Each step was bringing her closer to him, and the world was newly beautiful.

2

I was listening to this account in the corner booth of an otherwise empty tavern. I had arranged this meeting; in fact, I'd been compelled to arrange it and now I was blowing off the whole afternoon for it.

The young woman across from me had blindsided me during my last trial, in a way nothing else had in my entire legal career. There are many reasons I'm considered one of the best defense attorneys in Kings County, and one of them is my ability to anticipate every aspect of a courtroom battle.

My first boss—Milton Willis—was a master of litigation and he molded me in his own image. A heavy glass paperweight on his desk was inscribed with these words: *For every hand extended, another lies in wait.* It was a line from a song called *Anticipate.*

His rules were fixed and inflexible, and I thought of them every day. *Never ask a question in a trial unless you already know the answer. Never create an opening for the unexpected. Control every aspect of what unfolds on your watch.*

Whenever I thought I was on top of any and every possibility, he would urge me to think again. *This is a complicated game*, he liked to say, *and there are sixty-four squares on the chessboard.*

This was guidance I lived by, and by the time I strode into the courtroom on expensive heels and said, "My name is Lillian Reeve and I represent Abel Nathanson," I believed I had a true blueprint of every box on the board before me.

Nan had obliterated this conviction and dealt a hard blow to my confidence. I needed to understand what happened.

I was dressed down for this encounter, in jeans and a gray t-shirt. I was trying for a vibe that was casual and cozy, one that would lower her guard. When the waitress came over, I asked for a French onion soup and a beer.

But Nan ordered nothing. She sat across from me in the dimly lit booth, her back perfectly straight. She wore a high-necked blouse with a bow at the throat and she held herself still as she spoke. Her gaze was direct and her presence unsettling.

A few days earlier, when I'd called to ask whether we could meet, she had astonished me by saying, "I'll only talk with you if we can officially deem the meeting a *pro bono* legal consultation. You'll need to sign something to that effect. I need an airtight assurance of confidentiality."

I remembered the first time I met her. Abel had been indicted the day before. He was at the firm to retain my services. Nan was at his side; he held her arm with one hand, his cane with the other.

They were a striking pair. Despite his odd facial disfigurement and his blindness, there was something suave about him, an air of serene self-possession. And her looks were arresting; she was slender and delicate with wide gray eyes and the innocent gaze of some woodland creature. Improbably proper, even prim, and yet I could sense an abject yearning beneath her composure, an unseemly need having to do with her boss. I wondered if they were sleeping together.

At the conference room table, she took a slate and stylus from her shoulder bag, along with a legal-sized manila folder. Written on its tab was the name of our firm, *Reeve and Rezac*, and beneath that was—presumably—the Braille translation. As I passed him written materials, Nan affixed them to her slate and created a tactile label for each one: the firm brochure, a retainer agreement, a breakdown of the various fees he might incur. She maintained the same impeccable posture in my office as here in the tavern: spine straight, shoulders set, even as she labored over the paper. She was the very picture of intelligence and competence, and fleetingly I wondered why she had chosen such a servile line of work. But then, I saw this all the time: young women who could do anything but were apparently content to assist some man.

I had never met Abel, but I'd heard of him. As the city's only non-profit industrial developer—and blind to boot—he was often in the local news. And until now, it had all been good press. He was known for reinventing the most unlikely build-ings (a former rope factory, a defunct armory, an abandoned cathedral) and making them newly beautiful and serviceable, usually to the benefit of some downtrodden sector. One of them, I didn't remember which, was now a charter school for autistic children.

"So, Mr. Nathanson," I said, when we were seated at the conference table. "To what do I owe the honor?"

"Well, to put it bluntly," he said, "I fucked up. Badly. What I did is frankly indefensible. I don't imagine there's much chance of being cleared of the charges against me. But I am looking for damage control, insofar as that might be possible. And I very much hope to avoid even a brief stint in prison."

"I'd like to assist with both of those goals," I said, in the calm voice I reserved for such moments, when a client is laying the broken pieces of his life before me and begging for some mea-sure of restoration.

"I've figured out what happened," Abel went on. "And there's no doubt I was set up. That doesn't excuse my actions. It just explains how I got caught so fast."

"Please tell me the story," I said.

"Well, first let me ask: do you know who John Bonney is?"

"The real estate developer?"

"Yes. Good. All right, so more than two years ago, he and I were vying for the same piece of the Brooklyn Navy Yard. I'd been a thorn in his backside many times before, but I don't think he seriously hated me until I won that bid. He was the city's favorite son for a long time, for reasons I probably don't need to break down for you."

"Well, I know he has deep pockets and a lot of…influence," I said.

"Yes. He's bankrolled a lot of political careers on the local level. It was easy to be cynical whenever the mayor handed him civic development projects and city-owned properties. By contrast, I was the kind of underdog that no one begrudged: young, blind, self-made, in the non-profit sector. I've heard that, in Bonney's inner circle, they call me *Poster Boy*."

"Well, that's not very nice," I said. "Though I've been called worse." I was trying to put him at ease. His blindness complicated this: he couldn't see the framed credentials on my wall, the posh decor of my corner office, the framed desk photos of my infant niece and childhood dog. (For building rapport with a new client, I'd found that nothing was better than a picture of a dog.) And it worked. The corner of his mouth went up in a half-smile and I realized I liked him. It wasn't essential to like my clients—and often I didn't—but it helped.

"Anyway," Abel went on. "Within the last six months, we both submitted proposals for the Red Hook waterfront. That's really what this is all about. Bonney was afraid that history would repeat itself, and he wanted to knock me out of the running."

"And how did he do that?" I asked, pen poised over a legal tablet.

"Well, soon after we submitted competing proposals for the property, a firm called Apex, which I'd never worked with, started to court me very aggressively. The rep's name was Tom Roscoe and the bids he submitted to me should have been a red flag, because they were very, very low. Too low. He undercut his competitors' rates by so much that it made me wonder how the hell his firm would have a profit margin."

"And?" I said.

"Well, a little digging, far too late, reveals that Roscoe's not even a full-time employee at Apex. He just moonlights there from time to time because he's the owner's nephew. His real job is with the NYPD. He's a cop. But here's the best part. The boss over at Apex—Roscoe's uncle? He's Bonney's brother-in-law."

"So you think the whole bid was a ruse."

"There's no doubt in my mind. They wanted to get me into bed with Roscoe so he could rake up some muck. And I cringe to think about how fast he managed that."

Abel paused in the telling. Beside him, Nan was composed and still, eyes cast downward. Still, there was something in her bearing that made it plain to me: she was as pained by this situation as if she were his wife.

"Please go on," I said.

"Okay, well, I won't go into the whole sob story, but around this time my sister was in serious financial straits. She's a single mom with a special-needs kid and caring for him is a full-time job. She's always scrambling around for work she can do from home after he goes to bed, like stuffing envelopes or data entry. As you can imagine, it's brutal. She's always exhausted, always broke, but things were at an all-time low after she bought this disaster of a house a few miles upstate."

As Abel went on, a bleak story emerged: of a struggling mother in a house she'd gotten dirt-cheap because so much was wrong with it. A house that kept flooding, kept failing her.

"She needed to replace the roof, put in a new septic tank and field…I mean, we're talking about tens of thousands of dollars. I've given her money before, lots of times, but it humiliates her to take it. And I knew that this time it would all but kill her, because I told her not to buy that house.

"So when I heard Roscoe's miraculous rates, I couldn't help thinking of her," Abel continued. "I asked whether Apex did any residential work, and when Roscoe said yes, I wanted to know what it would cost to rehab her house on the side. Of course, even this was sheer idiocy—someone in my position doesn't use the same vendor for public and private work. But what did me in was my response to what he said next.

"He basically told me: *Hey look, you give us the big job, and not only will I give you a great deal on your sister's house, but if you want, I can bury those charges in the Navy Yard invoice.*" Abel exhaled sharply. "So—do you follow? The Navy Yard project's a multi-million-dollar tab. An extra thirty or forty thousand wouldn't even be noticeable. I figured the city would pay it without looking twice. And so, God help me, I took him up on this offer."

"Ah," I said, quietly.

"You have to understand—dangling this kind of carrot is absolutely standard in the industry. All contractors offer you this stuff off the back of the truck. But as someone entrusted with public capital, I can't afford to reach for any of it, ever. And I never have before. I've returned *Christmas* bottles of *champagne* from corporate vendors, for Christ's sake. It was a one-time, disastrous lapse of judgment."

"You know," I said, half to myself, "I'm surprised the D.A. is going after this full throttle. Of course what you did was wrong, but as you've said, this kind of thing goes on every minute. Why now, why you? Does Kamin just want to make an example of someone? Even if that's his motive, I find you an unlikely choice."

"Kamin's planning a mayoral run next year," Abel said. "My guess is there's an understanding that Bonney will fill his campaign coffer one way or another. Aboveboard or under the table."

We sat in silence for a moment.

"If what you've said is true," I said slowly, "if a cop had a hand in setting you up, then an entrapment defense is one potential strategy."

"Avoiding prison is my main goal," Abel said. "If an entrapment defense would accomplish that, then I'm all for it. That won't restore my reputation, of course, but I suppose there's no hope of that anyway."

"No," I agreed. "But by explaining your sister's situation, we can tell a sympathetic and somewhat mitigating story. The fact is that you did what most people would do. We can't make it right, but we can make it understandable."

Now, in the tavern, I asked Nan, "How did you come to live at the convent?"

"It's one of those stories you hear about but don't think are real: as a baby, I was left on the doorstep of a Carmelite convent."

Oh, *come on*, I wanted to howl. Who was this preposterous woman? It was possible that everything she was telling me was a lie. As she herself had suggested, it was even possible that she was mentally ill. Nonetheless, I managed to keep my tone neutral. "Aren't the Carmelites a reclusive order?"

"Yes, they are. But the fold includes several externs who see to the day-to-day business of running the convent. They live in a separate annex and they're the ones who take care of the orphans."

"All right," I said. My soup had gone cold, and now I pushed the bowl away. "So how did you come to know Braille?"

"I taught it to myself," she answered.

"Just for Abel?" It was an inane question. She'd already told me she had never before known anyone who was blind.

"Yes, of course."

"Did he ask you to learn it?"

"No, he never did," she said. "I just thought I should."

My initial meeting with Abel took place late on a Friday afternoon. He was my last appointment of the day and snow was falling when I left the office afterward.

I was troubled about a tense exchange I'd had with the receptionist on my way out. The phones were quiet as I passed her desk and she was reading a book. Beneath the title on the cover—*The Prince's Captive*—was a woman with windswept hair in the embrace of a bare-chested man, and I felt an ancient irritation flare within me.

"Penny," I said. "Outside the workplace, your choice of reading material is of course your own. But when you're here, you are representing this firm, and *that*…"—I pointed at her book—"…is not appropriate for the office."

My partner Dana walked by us and out the door, with a slight wave and a glance I couldn't read. But when I joined her at the elevator bank, she gave me a dubious look. "Really, Lil," she said. "She's the receptionist. Who cares if she reads a bodice-ripper during the slow hours? What do you want her to look at, a law journal?"

"Dana, I've worked hard to build a serious practice. First impressions are important. I'll be damned if clients walk into this firm and the first thing they see is trash like that."

Dana sighed. She was used to me. "Anyway, have a good weekend," she said, squeezing my shoulder at the building exit.

Once on the street, I thought about walking four blocks out of my way to the nearest gourmet market for brie and a bottle of Chardonnay. That was the kind of thing I did when Darren and I were first married. But by now, I tended to see such efforts as a contrivance. A way of trying to make our life look the way I thought it should: the power couple with the hot marriage.

For years now, whenever we resolved to have a romantic evening—breaking out the wine and building a fire in the fireplace—it felt as if we were just going through the motions so that we could congratulate ourselves afterward. Because, really, I was thinking about my work and he was thinking about his.

A counselor once told us to make a ritual of connecting when we got home from work. And we tried to heed this advice. He'd make himself ask about my day and I'd do the same, but we were like two diligent students completing an assignment. It was a relief when we let it go.

Tonight Darren was already on his way out as I was coming in. He was putting on his coat when I walked through the door.

"Where are you going?" I asked.

"I told you I was seeing Reg tonight." Reg was his college roommate who occasionally came to town on business.

"You did not."

"Yes, Lil. I did."

"Well, how late are you going to be?"

"I really don't know. I think he and Tina are going through a rough time, maybe even looking at divorce. He might want to talk for a while. So don't wait up."

This was a joke. I never waited up for Darren.

"All right, but that means we have to do it now."

"Do what now?"

"I don't know why I ever expect you to know, since you can't be bothered to glance at the ovulation calendar, but it's that time."

"Oh come on, Lil. I told him I'd see him in twenty minutes."

"Well, tell him you'll see him in twenty-five."

I kicked off my shoes, moved down the hall to the bedroom, stripped off my skirt and stockings and lay back on the bed. He appeared in the doorway.

"Listen, I was seriously just on my way out."

"This doesn't have to take long."

"Christ," Darren said. He threw his coat on the bed and stripped from the waist down. "I resent the hell out of this, all right? Just so you know. I feel like a fucking stud horse."

"Yeah, it's so tough having a wife who demands sex. You know, a lot of guys would be happy to have this problem," I said.

"And I might be happy too, if I thought you weren't just in it for the jizz. If the whole thing weren't all business."

He sat on the edge of the bed, using his hand to work himself up.

"Look, if you weren't in a rush, I wouldn't be like this. I just don't want to make you later than necessary."

Darren didn't answer. He had achieved an erection and he wordlessly mounted me. Despite my urgency, I myself wasn't ready and it hurt, but I gritted my teeth and resolved to ignore the pain.

In. Out. In. Out. What an overrated activity. After several long minutes, I actually looked at my watch. What if after all this, he couldn't get off? That happened once in a while. "Darren, are you...are you close?" I asked.

"Can you get on your hands and knees?" he asked. It was his favorite position, or one of them. I didn't like it, or at least, didn't like the fact that I liked it.

"Missionary works best for conception," I told him. "Next time we can do it your way."

I'd almost said "next month," and while I was glad I hadn't, it wouldn't have been inaccurate. We had sex when the calendar demanded, and that was it.

Eight more wordless minutes passed before I got what I wanted, and two minutes after that, he was gone. I stayed in bed, holding the position I'd been advised to try, knees bent, hips thrust skyward, feeling forlorn. The beauty of the snow falling outside the window only sharpened this sadness.

I wondered what to do about dinner. I began to wish I'd bought that bottle of wine, though drinking alone was hardly an uplifting prospect. I thought of calling Leda but ever since she'd had her own baby, it had become harder to take comfort from our conversations. There was a peace in her voice that had never been there before and I wanted to feel glad about that. But all I could feel was a suffocating jealousy. Along with a stung mystification: we were physically identical, or nearly so, so why had Leda conceived within weeks of getting married, while I had been trying for years?

And just then, the phone rang and it was her. This had happened all of our lives. I would think about calling her and the phone would ring. Everyone always said it must be a twin thing, and maybe it was. While I was wavering over whether to answer, the machine picked up and I heard her voice on the recorder.

"Lily, call me, I have some great news—"

She couldn't possibly be pregnant again yet. Could she? Heart pounding, I snatched the phone from its cradle.

"Leda?"

"Hey! Screening your calls?"

"I just—I was in the other room and I didn't get to the phone in time."

She wasn't pregnant again. (Thank God.) The news was that she and her husband were buying a house in Washington. They would be moving just across the river from their current rental in Portland, Oregon.

"Oh," I said, relieved and ready to be excited for her. "That's wonderful, Leda. You know, Darren and I have been talking about seeing his dad in Calgary, and visiting that part of Canada. Maybe we can fly into Portland to help you move and then drive north. This might be what'll get us in gear to really do it."

As I proposed this, I felt cheered for the first time since coming home. To me, there was nothing more romantic than a road trip. Maybe that was what Darren and I needed right now.

"Oh, Lily, that would be great. The actual move won't be for another few months—we didn't want to break our lease, and the owners agreed to wait till May. Could you come then?"

"I'll have to check Darren's schedule, but I think May could work, actually. Maybe around Memorial Day weekend? Of course, we might need to renew our passports. I'll have to look."

We talked for a while longer, mostly about the new house, and I felt a surge of the old comfort that, until recently, I'd always taken from hearing her voice.

And then I hung up and went into my husband's study and opened his file cabinet in search of our passports and that's when I saw it.

First: a glimpse of an image I registered as illicit before I even knew what I was looking at. A flash of black leather straps crisscrossing a woman's body—an otherwise naked body. It was in an unmarked folder at the back of the drawer. It was a pornographic DVD.

This was shocking in itself. Darren was well aware of my opposition to porn. In law school, I wrote arguments in support of a federal law banning it from the internet and I'd presented at conferences about the link between the porn industry and human trafficking. Darren had always expressed support for

my views. For a moment I thought maybe this DVD had something to do with one of his cases, though there was no legal
material in the folder, no correspondence or notes, nothing
else at all. Then I lifted it out and the shock of what I saw was
like a blow to the throat. I almost dropped the box.

Because the woman on the cover was me.

It wasn't me, of course. But the amended reality, which asserted itself a moment later, was nearly as impossible to take in.
It was Leda.

Her hair was blonde—an obvious dye job—and her eyes
were blue, whether from colored contacts or photo retouching,
I couldn't tell. But it was her. The copyright date was 1991, the
year Leda was nineteen. (The year *we* were nineteen.) What
had I been doing the year she made this movie? I'd had an
internship in Boston, at the Exoneration Project, a group dedi-
cated to seeking the reversal of wrongful convictions. Leda
never said a word about it to me.

Her real last name was not on the box. The cover read:
Introducing Leda Swann.

I stood there for several moments, holding it gingerly, as if it
were a grenade. I didn't want to know anything more about it; I
certainly didn't want to watch it. I wished I hadn't found it at
all, wished I were the kind of woman who would drop it back
into the folder, close the drawer, and find a way to pretend
never to have seen it in the first place. But I wasn't that woman,
and no form of clarity—however awful—had ever been worse
than my imagination.

I put the disc in the DVD player and sat at the edge of the
couch. My knees were pressed together and I was clasping my
own arms for warmth, though the apartment was overheated.
As the movie played, my chill deepened and at one point I
had to pause the video to grab a blanket from the linen closet.

I was shivering by the time the credits came onscreen, nearly feverish.

The…heroine? of the film was Jenny J., who has made a career of marrying for money. Her several husbands have all been wealthy and too old to be a nuisance for long. Naturally a woman like that needs some action on the side, so Jenny gets it on with the pool guy—a fine specimen of manhood with a penchant for leather and head games (vaguely recognizable to me as a boyfriend Leda had at the time). As promised in the copy on the back of the box, it's not long before Jenny gets her cumuppance, in the form of sexual slavery. With the pool man as master, overseer and inheritor-by-proxy.

I'd never watched a movie like this before, not for lack of opportunity, of course, but by choice, adamant choice. And if ever I'd wondered whether I might be missing something, well, now I had an unequivocal answer. The whole thing was an infuriating affront: the sordid story line and crude dialogue; the artlessness, inanity, misogyny.

Leda. *Leda. My* sister, with her beauty and talent, her fine mind and formidable charisma. *This* was what she had chosen to do with all of that?

And suddenly I could hear her voice in my head, clear and cool and amused: *Would you get a fucking grip, sister-love? I was nineteen years old and it was one week out of my life.*

And of course this was true. So why did the idea of this single youthful indiscretion make me crazy? It wasn't just that she'd taken such a degrading role. It was something else, something unmistakable about her performance: the fact that she'd loved playing that part, *loved* it.

I restarted the DVD and was halfway through the second viewing when Darren walked into the room. I hadn't heard his key in the front lock, hadn't heard his footsteps.

He stared at the screen for a moment, then dropped onto the far end of the couch. "Ah, Christ," he said.

How long have you had this?

A long time.

I never even knew Leda did this. Why didn't you tell me?

Because I knew how you'd react.

You! With all your supposed support for my activism, after the countless times you've agreed that porn demeans all of us, that it's linked to human trafficking, that it's woman-hating and…and alienating and…

Yes, you see, this is why I never felt I could tell you.

So how long have you had the hots for Leda?

I don't. Really. I mean, I know how it looks, but I'm not attracted to Leda. I never have been. I don't know how to explain it, but you need to believe this—it's about you, not her.

Oh, come on, Darren! I'm sorry to break this to you, but that…is…not…me!

I know that. But I guess it's just…my fantasy of some secret side of you, or something.

When we finally got into bed, I moved as far away from my husband as I could and lay on my side, facing the wall. Darren put a hand on my back but I jerked away.

"Don't touch me," I said.

He withdrew his hand and didn't try again.

My good feeling about Leda was irretrievable, at least for now, and I didn't even mention the idea of visiting her. My thoughts kept wandering to certain scenes between my sister and her old boyfriend and then eventually, inexplicably, to my blind client and his assistant. After a while, I realized that the aura—an annoying, new-age word but I couldn't find a better one—around Leda in the movie was something like the aura around Nan: a force field of whole-hearted focus, devotion, self-abandonment. Rapture.

3

Even after several months in Abel's office, it was hard for Nan to believe that she could be with him full-time, and often her workday was like a dream of floating above the floor. She would find her rhythm before the coffee was brewed, put in a full day's work by noon, anticipate what Abel wanted before he asked for it. He'd call her into his office to read, then ask, "Would you mind getting me a cup of coffee before we start?"

"I brought one in with me, Abel, it's right here."

There were glorious moments, like the one that came several weeks into the job, when Abel's notes to himself came off his printer and she read the top line out loud without thinking. "Bedford construction postponed until March?"

Abel went very still for a moment before half-turning in his chair. *"Do you know Braille?"*

"Well," she said. "I'm learning it. At least I'm trying to learn it."

"For what?"

"Just because I—I imagined it could be useful to you."

There was another pause. Then, in a dry tone that meant he was more pleased than he was willing to let on, he said, "I imagine it could be."

And it was useful, it was continually useful. At outside meetings, whenever written materials were distributed, she took out her metal slate and transcribed them for him on the spot. She labeled his file folders, slipped him notes while he was on the phone, and even made the office calendar—where everyone's schedule was posted—accessible to him.

Braille was harder to learn than Nan had imagined. Before she knew anything about it, she thought it was just a matter of mastering the alphabet. But there were hundreds of symbols to memorize, symbols that stood for whole words or letter combinations, more symbols still to denote capital letters and punctuation marks and italics, and rules for their use that were anything but intuitive. To create the raised print using her stylus, she had to work from the reverse side of the paper, across the page from right to left, with each letter rendered as its own mirror image.

She worked on her Braille every night. Whatever issued from Abel's thunderous printer and was later discarded, she took out of the trash and brought home with her. The better part of each evening was spent at her desk, bent over these documents with her transcriber's guide. The circle of lamplight cast her silhouette on the wall and surrounded it like a halo as she pored over the near-invisible text, the pages of white on white.

And sometimes her workday was like a long swallow of something bitter. One of the worst days—she could see this now, though she hadn't then—had to do with Abel's crime.

"Nan," he said that morning, on his way past her desk, "I need a copy of what you sent the board of directors yesterday. The final version of the Roscoe estimate."

And opening the file folder, Nan realized the mistake she'd made the day before.

"Oh no," she said, half to herself.

Abel turned back to face her. "What is it?"

"I just realized I did something wrong."

He stood there, waiting, and she saw his knuckles whiten around the top of his cane.

"I'm sorry," Nan added, still staring at the papers in her hand. "I don't know how it happened."

"Well, why don't you tell me what you did?"

She realized then that he was afraid—more afraid than the situation seemed to warrant—but reining himself in so she would tell him what she'd done, which broke her heart because she would tell him anyway, she would never withhold the truth from him, no matter what the cost to herself. But his reaction was making her, in turn, more frightened than she'd ever been in that office, and she had no idea what was at stake—had she incriminated him in some way? betrayed him?—so her confession came haltingly.

"I—by accident I…sent them the signed original. Not the copy."

"Oh," he said, and exhaled, and even in her state she could tell it was an exhalation of relief. "I thought you were going to tell me you sent the earlier version."

"No," she told him. "No, I sent the most recent version. Definitely."

"I was trying to decide whether to fire you on the spot, or take you into my office and fire you," he said.

It took Nan a moment to make sense of this.

"Are you…" The words were like a bone in her throat; she had to stop and swallow hard. "Are you serious?"

"As the day is long."

Tears came into her eyes and for once she was grateful that he couldn't see, more grateful still that no one else was around.

"Oh," she said finally.

"There are some mistakes," he said, "that you can't make."

And he walked away.

Later that afternoon, the door opened and his four-year-old daughter Lulu ran past the reception area. She was trailed by Deirdre, who was still lovely at forty-two, with silver threading her long dark hair, and eyes that made Nan think of Monet's water lilies.

Lulu paused at the threshold to Abel's office. Then with exaggerated stealth, she sneaked across the room, darted behind his desk, and shrieked, "Boo!" Nan had never seen Abel laugh harder than he did then. He grabbed the little girl up in a hug and cradled her in his arms before setting her down again.

But most of the hard days contained nothing so dramatic. More often, they were just empty of real contact with him. Every employee in the office would claim his time, one after the next, and he'd have no immediate need for her. She'd listen to him talking on the phone, sometimes with a special warmth he reserved for certain women. Eight hours could go by in which he barely spoke to her.

It was so important, she thought, not to look back, but once in a while, during these unyielding hours, some memory of the Nutcracker would come to her. A class ring on a man's hand could remind her, a hint of aftershave or maybe a certain accent. At those times, she couldn't help craving the luxury of such an explicit understanding.

The drawl of the fax repairman made her think of the Texan and his laconic threats. *I'm gonna tan your hide*, he used to tell her. *I'm gonna wear you out.*

There was more than one way to wear someone out. Not doing what you longed to do, what you were meant to do, could wear a person out. It was a daily and wearying effort to be on her feet in Abel's presence, to call him by his given name instead of *sir*.

Whenever she came up hardest against that wall, life inside the convent could seem like another enviable arrangement. Anyone who believed the sisters had sacrificed their earthly lives for an uncertain hereafter had never known the joy of worship. To understand that the nuns were already living in a better world was to recognize a literal truth. The brides of Christ were never forsaken or alone; they were always beholden, always beheld. They shared the assurance that no act of devotion, however private, was lost on the most important witness. And love came to them in a ceaseless stream: every sunrise was a benediction, each snowflake a kiss.

Nan understood this now. It was like that every weekday morning when she walked to work; the beauty of that first morning had never faded. Each city block held something lovely to look at: green tendrils twining along a barbed wire fence, a red embroidered mitten dropped on the sidewalk, jeweled pastries in a bakery window. The world was brimming over with beauty and she could see it everywhere, because she belonged to Abel.

Harsh weather never kept her from walking. Coming into the office out of the rain or sleet had its own special appeal. Abel was warmth, he was shelter, as sure as he was her touchstone and her rosary. She loved to strip off her wet coat and drape it over the radiator, shake off her umbrella, heat a pot of water for tea.

Walking home in the evening was bittersweet. She was never more aware of the miracle of sight than when she had just spent eight to ten hours in Abel's domain. Outside, the twilight was tender, dreamy, laden with mystery. Sometimes she stood there a moment just taking it in: the sky like a child's chalk drawing, the branches etched against it, the patina of steeples in the distance. Clothes fluttered like flags on their lines, linking one building to another.

The day Roscoe made his fateful offer to Abel was as vivid in her memory as if it were yesterday. He had been to the office many times by then, with his own assistant in tow: a young woman roughly Nan's age. Erica.

They arrived that morning for a meeting with Abel. Nan brought both of them coffee in the reception area. Then she went to Abel's office to let him know they'd arrived.

Abel liked to make people wait.

"I want Matt at this meeting too," he said, referring to his project manager. "You can get him when I'm ready. In the meantime..." he held up one of the papers from the stack on his desk. "What's this?"

"That's your fax from Ken Cartwright."

"Okay. And this?"

"It's your letter to Mandy Yee."

"Great, that's what I wanted. I need you to fax a copy to Phil"—Phil was Abel's planning director—"and send it out to her today."

"Someone's coming to repair the fax machine at eleven," she told him. "In the meantime, may I have you sign it?"

"Oh. Yeah. Good point."

This was a rare chance to touch him. She put a pen into his hand, placed her own hand over his, and set it directly on the line. His signature was nothing more than a jagged wave, but those who knew it could still tell the difference between the real thing and a forgery.

It was at least ten minutes before Abel summoned Matt and went out with him to the reception area. Nan watched Erica kiss Matt's cheek and then waver over whether to do the same with Abel. In the social arena, so much physical contact relied on visual cues—intentions signaled in advance, consent sought and granted, as one person leaned in and the other bent in reception. Who would dare such an intimate gesture without implicit permission? Not Erica. So often, amidst these exchanges, Abel was set apart, an island—as if blindness warranted a kind of quarantine.

But the truth was that Nan was grateful for people's reluctance to touch him. She didn't know how much of it she could stand. She was jealous enough—jealous of everyone else whose arm he took; jealous of the dog, who was free to follow him from room to room; even jealous of the man she'd read about in the paper, who donated a kidney to his boss. She dreamed of a situation in which she could do the same for Abel: give him her kidney, her blood, her bone marrow, her breath. This, she knew, was how the nuns felt about Christ, and what the church said He felt for his human flock. It made His endurance easier to fathom. There must have been at least a moment, hanging there, when He was beyond exhaustion, beyond pain, hovering above His executioners, high enough to see for miles. Drunk on the grandiosity of His gesture, arms nailed forever open.

When Abel asked Tom Roscoe about the repairs to his sister's house, Erica was in the ladies' room and Matt was outside making a call. The conference room door was slightly ajar and Nan, on her way to tell Abel that his next appointment had arrived, overheard this exchange between the two men:

"…if you want, I can bury those charges in the Navy Yard invoice." This was Roscoe, speaking low.

And then there was a long startled pause before Abel said, "Now that's an idea."

("What did you think, when you heard that?" I asked Nan in the tavern.

"It really wasn't my place to think anything.")

4

I hardly spoke to my husband during the week that followed my discovery of Leda's movie. And for several days I didn't talk to my sister either, though she called to check in about our proposed visit and left at least two messages. I stayed late at the office, digging into the past of John Bonney, a frustrating endeavor. Other than a few IRS audits and a paternity suit (filed against him and thrown out in short order), there wasn't much on the guy.

Abel and Nan came in once during this time. While Nan went out to pick up the Japanese takeout we would have for lunch, Abel filled me in on his formidable career. During the trial, I would need to cast him as a hero and he made it easy. There were the countless artisans and craftsmen—many of them first-generation Americans, skilled in some old-world trade—who would have been mopping floors or working the deep fryer at some fast-food joint if it weren't for the subsidized space provided by Abel. There were the historic buildings, condemned by the city and slated to be torn down, that he saved and renovated. He was a tireless champion of the city's endangered manufacturing sector. He'd saved and created hundreds of jobs. He gave money to many causes, including the National Federation of the Blind, the Guide Dog Foundation and the American Association of People with Disabilities. He had adopted a Romanian orphan.

Nan returned with a paper bag and, without a word, began setting its contents on the conference table: three bento boxes, napkins and several sets of chopsticks. Then she took the lid off

Abel's box, placed his tray in front of him, and spoke low near his ear.

"Chopsticks are on the left, maki in front of you, edamame on the lower right and the soy sauce just above that."

"Thank you, Nan."

Watching them, I remembered the first time they came in, and how I'd wondered if they were sleeping together. For some reason, I was now sure that they weren't, and yet I still had the sense that this young woman spent her every working hour in a kind of erotic trance.

What else could account for the serenity that seemed to radiate from her? Her job involved no glory. It would lead to nothing better and it surely didn't pay much. And yet I was only more certain as time went on that she had something I didn't: a certain kind of fulfillment I'd never known and might never know.

I married my best friend. And I know that sounds enviable. Darren was in my class at the University of Chicago Law School and we did everything together: studied for the bar exam, ran along the river, worked the Sunday *New York Times* crossword in bed. I was only twenty-four on our wedding day. Leda, of course, was my maid of honor.

In our family, I was the worker bee—diligent and reliable—while Leda was the firefly, glittering and unpredictable. She got more attention and I got more approval. My boyfriend in high school was my debate team partner, a serious young man named Daniel who went on to Harvard; we were together from sophomore year through graduation. Leda had a string of romances. She dated the star of the senior class play and the captain of the basketball team and a drummer who went on to modest fame in an indie grunge band. Her college experience wasn't much of a departure from this pattern. She broke a lot of hearts and had her heart broken too.

After graduating law school with highest honors, Darren and

I married and moved to New York City, where we settled in an apartment near Lincoln Center. We spent the next several years working the long hours of ambitious, dues-paying associates at two of the city's top law firms.

Leda, on the other hand, wanted to be an actress. She moved to L.A. and worked at a string of dispensable jobs while landing various acting roles that paid little to nothing. She fell in love with a cast of dubious characters, both onstage and off. And apparently she'd had at least a brief stint as a porn star.

That movie. *Payback*. In the week since discovering it, I'd watched it at least half a dozen times. Darren had kept it a secret from me and now I kept my preoccupation with it a secret from him. Something about it would not let me put it aside.

Leda looked beautiful in the movie. Even blonde and blue-eyed, she was still like a wanton, wayward version of me. Watching it felt wildly uncomfortable, compromising.

Once during our high school years, I came into the bedroom I shared with Leda to see her diary lying open on the floor beside her desk, where it must have fallen. I had no intention of reading it but I caught sight of my name and couldn't look away. *I've always been sexually open and free, whereas Lillian is very private and somewhat repressed,* she had written. This assessment haunted me constantly during the days and weeks that followed.

Some time later, during a fight about my refusal to tell her the details of what I did with Daniel—this was after she called me withholding, called me a prig—I sneered, "Well, not everyone can be as *open and free* as you. Some of us are *repressed.*"

"Bloody hell, Lillian," she said. (She was dating a British exchange student at the time.) "You read my journal. That would kill me, if it were anyone but you."

I thought of denying it, but knew it was useless. "Why is it less awful that it's me?" I asked instead.

"You know why. Because of how it is with us. You know that wretched phrase, *my better half,* which is supposed to be about your husband? No man could ever be that to me, Lily. Because that's you, and it will always be you."

Another time, deep in a pot haze—this was in our late twenties—she intoned, "It's like we're one person split in two. I got the wildness, the darkness and the artistry."

It was all I could do not to roll my eyes. "And?" I demanded when she said nothing further. "What did I get?"

"You got the credentials, the integrity and the sense."

But after an extended youth of doing exactly as she pleased, Leda was engaged and then married and then pregnant in less time than it took for an average case of mine to come to trial. Meanwhile all the doctors Darren and I consulted over the years found no reason for our failure to conceive, but at this point we pretty much expected to remain childless. Of course, like Abel and his wife, we could have adopted, and perhaps we would yet. But by now, our childlessness had permitted a full-bore professional intensity for so long that we both had a prized place in the legal firmament and we both liked it there very much. Even as I made myself a slave to the ovulation calendar, the idea of having a baby became less and less imaginable.

In the meantime, the sex between us had long been stripped of the spontaneity and joy of our early years. Now it was fraught with shame and sorrow, a pervasive sense of failure.

5

Somewhere within the dream of slavery is the dream of adoption: of being taken off the auction block, taken home. Perhaps this had something to do with the way Nan felt when her phone rang on a Sunday night in April, and it was Abel.

"I'd like you to come to the house tomorrow morning, instead of to the office," he told her. "Deirdre broke her right arm over the weekend. I'm going to try to work at home if I can. It would be great if you could read for me and then, if you don't mind, run a few errands for her."

For months after she started working in the office, the image of Abel's house had stayed with her like a faded snapshot, washed in sepia and stashed out of reach. And now, finally, here it was: her chance to return there. She told him she would be there by 9:00 A.M., then lay awake most of the night, staring into the darkness and trying to contain her anticipation.

When Abel let her in the next morning, he said, "There's coffee on the stove. Why don't you have a cup, and help yourself to whatever else you want. I have a few phone calls to make and then I'll be with you."

Nan went into the kitchen but instead of pouring herself coffee, she cleared the remains of breakfast from the table. She rinsed the dishes, wiped down the countertop, and was sweeping the floor when Deirdre spoke from the doorway. Her face was chalky with pain and her arm was in a sling.

"You're a real self-starter, aren't you," she said.

Her tone was so flat that Nan couldn't tell whether it held gratitude or censure.

"Oh, Deirdre, I'm so sorry about your arm," she said in a

rush. "Can I get you anything? Coffee or tea or…anything?"

"That's all right, I've had my breakfast. When you're ready, I can show you what needs to be done."

"I'm ready now," she said.

In the foyer, a stack of outgoing mail lay on a side table and a laundry bag had been left by the front door. Nan was to take the mail to the post office and the clothes to the cleaners. There were instructions for Abel's work shirts: pressed but not starched, and a button on one cuff that needed to be replaced. And there were two different shopping lists: one for the neighborhood co-op and one for the regular supermarket. Deirdre had written them with her left hand, in print as uncertain as a child's.

As she was going over these lists, a man with wild, matted hair and a grease-stained sweatshirt appeared in front of the house and began sweeping the walk. Through the open window Nan could hear him muttering to himself, a fierce monologue punctuated by strokes of the broom.

"Nan," Deirdre said. "Take five dollars out of my purse."

But as soon as she had done so, Abel called down from upstairs. "Don't talk to him and don't give him any money!"

Deirdre smiled at her and spoke in the lowered tone of conspiracy. "Honey, you run out and give him that."

Nothing in Nan's experience had prepared her for this moment. She stood rooted to the spot and felt her neck flush with distress.

"Go on," Deirdre urged. "It's all right. We go through this every morning. He's just fussing."

Nan didn't move. She wasn't afraid that Abel would really be angry. She understood that this was a ritual of theirs. But she could no more defy an order from Abel than she could grow a pair of wings. She stood looking at Deirdre helplessly, pleadingly.

"Oh, give it here," the other woman said finally, and took the money back. Nan heard her call out, "Good morning!" as she went down the front steps.

At the cleaners, before surrendering their clothes, Nan lifted one of Abel's shirts from the drawstring bag and pressed it to her face. Inhaling its scent—the tang of its last iron, a trace of talc and his own faint sweat—stopped her breath and tightened her throat. The clerk raised an eyebrow at her as he gave her the receipt.

At the health food store, Nan realized that much of what was on the list was just for Lulu. All-natural animal crackers and alphabet soup. Tiny ice cream sandwiches with frozen tofutti filling. Little boxes of juice individually wrapped with their own red-and-white-striped straws. Other items had been qualified with her in mind: "Bran cereal. No raisins," Deirdre had explained when going over the list with Nan. "We like raisins but Lulu won't touch them."

Abel had described Lulu's orphanage to Nan once: a place so primitive and understaffed that some of the kids were tied to the beds. Lulu was still a baby, only twelve weeks old.

"Did you pick her out right there?" Nan asked then. She knew there were still places in the world where children could be picked out like pets from the pound. It hardly made her sorry for Lulu. She couldn't imagine anything closer to heaven than being picked out by Abel and Deirdre. The two of them *wanted* Lulu, they crossed an ocean to get her, and they hadn't done it out of any sense of piety or charity.

"We had already picked her out," Abel told her. "We were there to pick her up."

In the dairy aisle, Nan found the brand of cream cheese that Deirdre had written down. On the box was a picture that might have come from one of Lulu's books: a cheerful cow jumping in a field of grass. The side panel promised that its ingredients were pure and no harm had come to any of the cows on their farm. It was cream cheese for a happy family in a sunlit kitchen, and the colors on the box blurred as Nan's eyes filled with tears.

At eight o'clock that evening, while Deirdre was putting Lulu to bed, Abel said, "Nan, thank you for everything you did today. I know this kind of work wasn't in your job description. It means a lot to me that you have this kind of flexibility."

She had eaten dinner with the family—a pizza she'd picked up on the next block. She wondered if they were going to be living on takeout for the next six weeks.

"I was happy to help you," she told him.

"I'll call you a car," he said. "Just tell the driver to put it on my account."

"Oh, no, please don't bother, the train's just two blocks away."

"I'm not going to have this conversation with you," Abel told her. "And listen, I might have you come back tomorrow. I'll call you in the morning and let you know."

The next night, she cooked for them—nothing complicated, just pasta with vegetables. Deirdre stood next to her and told her what to do. Nan was glad for her direction—cooking was a skill she had never learned. The nuns' meals were spare and plain, and the same sister was always responsible for them. Nan had never even been inside the convent kitchen.

After dinner, Abel said, "I'll call you another car. And to-morrow I should be back in the office. Just come in as usual unless you hear from me."

And then, as he moved toward the phone, Nan had a sudden inspiration.

"You know," she blurted to his back, "I've been meaning to ask—how have all of you been getting along in the mornings?"

Abel turned around. "Lulu's happy," he said. "She gets to eat Lucky Charms instead of oatmeal."

"What about you and Deirdre?"

When he didn't answer, Nan rushed in with what had come to her. "Listen…" she said. "It's so late, when I get home I'll just be going straight to bed. Is there any point in paying for a car? What if I just sleep on the sofa downstairs? That way I could get breakfast for everyone in the morning and ride into the office with you."

There was a silence. Abel seemed taken aback and Nan wondered if he could tell she was holding her breath.

Finally he said, "That's very kind of you. Really. But I couldn't ask you to do something like that."

"You didn't ask."

Deirdre leaned forward. "Oh, honey, bless your heart. But you've done so much for us already these two days. How could we let you go to any more trouble?"

"Nothing would be easier." Nan looked straight into Deirdre's eyes, saying this. "All I have to do is lie down and fall asleep."

6

By the end of the week, a routine was in place. In the morning, Nan made breakfast and ran errands for Deirdre: went to the bank, the cleaners, even the post office if anything had to be certified. She arrived in the office by 10:00 A.M. or so, and from that point on, she worked a regular day. At six o'clock, she rode home with Abel, cooked dinner, did the dishes, and brought Deirdre whatever she needed. She stopped by her apartment only once, over the weekend, to pick up some clothes and her toothbrush.

For the first few nights, it was hard for Nan to eat at the Nathansons' table. In the convent, meals were taken in silence, except for a recitation of Grace and a reading of Scripture by one of the nuns. Each sister ate whatever was put in front of her whether or not it was to her liking. Even crumbs were caught in a napkin and consumed—to waste the slightest amount was a sin against poverty.

In Abel's dining room, there was no form to observe, and therefore no way for Nan to relax. Still, within a few days, she was afraid of how good being there had begun to feel—even during the most difficult moments, like when Lulu looked up from her plate of ravioli and asked, "Is Daddy going to go away?"

A hush fell over the table.

Deirdre, who was sitting beside Abel, put a hand on his knee. She looked stricken. "Why do you ask that, honey?"

"Jack in my class said the police are going to put Daddy in jail."

"How would Jack know anything about Daddy?"

"He said his daddy read it in the newspaper."

Deirdre set her fork down. There was a tremor in her hand. "Jack has no way to know anything about what will or won't happen with Daddy."

"So the police aren't going to take Daddy away?" the little girl persisted.

There was a terrible silence and then Abel broke it. His voice was quiet and steady.

"Lulu, there's one thing I can promise you," he said. "No matter what happens, nothing in the world can take Daddy away from you. Even if we're separated for a little while."

"And Lulu, that's not likely to happen," Deirdre said in a rush.

"Did Daddy do something wrong?"

Deirdre shot a helpless glance at Abel, who responded in the same quiet tone. "Yes," he told her. "Daddy made a mistake."

"And Lulu, everyone makes mistakes. We've talked about that," Deirdre put in. "But a very smart lady is working to help Daddy stay out of jail. That's her job and she's very good at it."

"Oh," Lulu said, and went back to her ravioli.

Deirdre looked over at Nan with a mortified smile. *How awkward it must be*, that smile said, *for you, an outsider in the midst of all this*. Deirdre could always be counted upon to draw these lines, lest Nan start to feel like a part of the household.

Each night after dinner, Abel dried the dishes she had just washed and stacked them in the wooden rack. Nan loved standing next to him at the sink, close enough to feel his warmth, her arm occasionally brushing his. At these times, he still wore a work shirt, the sleeves rolled to the elbow, as he waited for her to put each plate into his outstretched hand.

What would she do if she belonged to them for all time?

Everything she was doing now, and anything else she could think of. She would buy the linen spray they were selling in the corner boutique and iron the scent of lilacs into their sheets. She would travel any distance to bring them whatever they wanted. She would babysit Lulu when they went out, take down the living room curtains and wash them, polish the silverware and dust the display china and scrub their hardwood floors.

And if Abel hadn't been a family man, and she belonged to him alone? She would rub him down with massage oil every night, bring him scotch in a shatterproof glass, read him his mail, screen his calls, and stay within easy reach.

("Was this the first time you ever lived with a family?"

"Yes. And it was also the first time I ever lived in a house."

"It must have been so different from what you were used to."

"Oh, more different than you could ever imagine.")

The rich femininity Deirdre brought to Abel's house fascinated Nan. The convent was so austere, and her own apartment didn't even look lived in. But in Deirdre's kitchen, ornamental bottles of cooking oil lined the windowsill. Bright red berries, lemon slices and whole jalapenos floated inside them as if trapped in amber. There was a hen-shaped wire basket for eggs, glass grinders of rock salt and peppercorns, a window box where herbs grew in little clay pots.

And then there were all the bottles and jars lining Deirdre's bathtub, with labels that read *milk bath*, *honeysuckle*, *tea rose*, *violet*, *jasmine*. There was the bed she shared with Abel, with its bank of lush pillows stacked against the headboard, its cream-colored down coverlet pulled tight over flannel sheets. There was a water glass and a stack of novels on her night table, loose change and a Braille-faced alarm clock on his.

At Our Lady of Sorrows, none of the sisters owned anything

but her sins. They used nothing besides their own homemade yellow soap when they bathed, and there were no mirrors on the wall of the communal washroom. Each sister had a gray-blanketed bed where she laid down her body and offered up her soul, along with a passion so ardent it could survive lifelong abstinence.

But looking at Deirdre's things, Nan could feel, for the first time, the seduction of luxury. There was a time when Deirdre's array of worldly goods would have struck Nan as vanity, frivolity, self-indulgence. But if she were married to a blind man like Abel and had the means, admittedly she would stop at nothing to delight all his other senses. Mary Magdalene broke her alabaster box to anoint Christ's feet, Christ himself turned water to the finest wine, and she thought Deirdre, at least, was doing the right thing.

("What did Deirdre think of you?"

"It's difficult to answer that. She was hard to read. I think she appreciated all my help. But she was bothered by the fact that I learned Braille for Abel."

"Oh?"

"She wished she'd thought of it herself. But it had never occurred to her.")

It was six weeks in, on a Thursday evening, when Nan was alone with Abel in the house for the first time. Deirdre had gone to a class, an art history course she was taking at the local college. Lulu had no school the next day and she was sleeping at the home of a friend. Abel was in the upstairs den with his contracts and leases, and when Nan went up to offer him a cup of tea, she found him asleep in his armchair.

His eyes were closed. She had wondered about that—whether blind people slept with their eyes closed. Standing there in the doorway, she was stunned by the privilege of the moment—the bluish shadows filling the room and the intimacy of watching him sleep.

She stepped over the threshold and did what she'd been longing to do since the morning she first came to his house. She knelt before his chair and as she did, she heard herself whimper. He stirred but did not open his eyes.

"Abel," she said in a hush.

He inhaled then as if rousing himself, and spoke quietly, but his eyes stayed closed.

"Yes," he said.

Nan continued to whisper, as if he were still asleep and she didn't want to wake him. "May I take your shoes off?"

There was a pause and then, "Yes," he said again, as if she'd asked him whether he wanted her to hold his calls.

She slowly tugged his laces from their knots, loosened his shoes, and pulled them off, revealing his feet in their black dress socks. She was breathing with an effort, her need rising inside her like floodwater.

Moments like these come suddenly and without warning, adrenaline-driven and past all decision, where no resistance is possible, no sense of propriety can prevail.

"Abel," she whispered once again.

"Mm."

She shut her own eyes now and pressed a fist to her mouth, cringing in disbelief. "May I…may I please kiss your feet?"

Then came the silence, the agonizing expected silence where she waited for him to open his eyes, struggle upright, make sure he'd heard right before putting as much distance between them as he could manage at the moment. But incredibly, after what seemed a considered pause, and with no particular surprise or alarm, he murmured in assent.

The men who came to the Nutcracker, they moved through the world without ever letting their secret desires break the surface of their daily lives. That's what Nan had been for: a visitation, a kind of angel, descended for an hour or a day, whatever they were willing to pay for. A commercial transaction, negotiated and contrived, but still better—or so they had decided—than waking up and going to sleep, year in and year out, without a flash of their deepest gratification in between. They were always married, to wives who wanted no part of this nonsense or possibly had no real idea what their husbands craved. Perhaps this was regrettable, or perhaps it was just wisdom. These passions, after all, aren't really made for this world.

It had been her job for so long to create and inhabit these spaces—just alongside of, but never quite touching, what everyone else called real life—that it shouldn't have been truly shocking to find herself here, stretched out face down on the floor, belly to the short stiff weave of the carpet, gripping Abel's ankles. But she was, she was shocked, she was trembling and overcome, terror giving slow way to gratitude as the minutes passed without retraction or retribution. She pressed her lips to the outline of each of his shrouded toes: first the left foot, then the right. After some time, she eased his socks off and lay there with her cheek to the bony plateau of his feet. Tears were leaking silently from her eyes and she let them trickle onto his warm skin.

In all this time, Abel had neither moved nor spoken. Was he some wayward counterpart to her, did this feel entirely right to him? So natural that there was no need to remark upon it? That was possible, and it was also possible that he was still asleep, and all of this was an intersection of his sleeping dream and her waking one.

After a while, she made herself get up and go back down-stairs, pausing at the doorway of the room to turn and whisper, *Good night*.

He and Deirdre went together to see her doctor the next morning, so for the first time in weeks, Nan walked to work. It had rained during the night and the wet streets held the sky's reflection. The city was shining, renewed, redeemed, and Nan was as happy as she had ever been.

She would often think of this morning, afterward. She would think of it as her last hours in Eden.

Around two o'clock that day, Abel summoned her to his office, and she went expecting to read the afternoon mail. Instead he pushed a check across the desk, made out for five thousand dol-lars in Matt's careful hand. Abel's own jagged signature was at the bottom. Nan was suddenly so afraid she could hardly speak.

"What is this?" she asked.

"Deirdre's sister is coming to town tonight," he told her. "She'll be staying with us through the end of next week. So she'll be able to help us out and Deirdre's cast is coming off on Monday anyway.

"Deirdre and I have talked it over," he continued, "and we both want to compensate you for all the extra time you put in at the house. It was an incredible gesture and we'll never forget it. Money isn't an adequate response to that kind of generosity, but we want to repay you in whatever way we can. I can only imagine how glad you'll be to finally go back home. But you've been as gracious as anyone could be. From both of us, thank you so very much."

There was a long silence while Nan tried to steady her breathing.

"Are you there?" Abel asked after a moment. It was a literal question.

"Yes, of course," Nan managed to say. "I'm sorry."

"Is something wrong?"

"I'm sorry, Abel."

"Nan," he said. "Are you…?"

For a moment, there was nothing but the sound of her weeping.

"What is it?" he asked. "Can you talk about it? Is there anything I can do?"

"Keep me," she heard herself say, knowing even in that moment that the words weren't going to stop this, weren't going to help in any way, and saying them left her hollow, like something crushed and empty by the side of the road. They represented a fatal loss of form, a stain on her record that would never stop spreading—never stop blackening what had been immaculate.

"What was that?" Abel asked after a moment. His tone was quiet and disbelieving. He was trying not to know what she couldn't keep from telling him. And once she started, she couldn't stop.

"Please," she whispered. Craven and begging. "Please let me stay with you."

There was a very long pause. Then:

"I don't understand," he said.

There are things too unbearable to think about, memories you can never let float into focus. Nan could barely bring herself to consider that day, and the terrible stilted awkwardness of the ones that followed, where she was unable to meet his sightless gaze and she knew things would never be the same. She seldom let herself remember how he decided within a week that he needed an assistant with a working knowledge of real estate. How he arranged for her to interview with the Lighthouse, a midtown non-profit providing services to the blind.

"We are in desperate need of sighted people who know Braille," the earnest, grandmotherly director told her when she went there. Abel predicted that they would pay her more than he had, and as with so many other things, he was right. She took the train to work now, and felt grateful when it was Friday like everyone else.

7

It was disconcerting the first time Abel came into my office without Nan. At her place by his side was a splendid German shepherd in a harness. I didn't yet know she was gone for good. I assumed she was out sick or maybe back at the office.

"What a beautiful dog," I said. I knew that only the owner was supposed to touch a guide dog, but I longed to stroke this one. "Where is Nan today?"

Abel seemed to hesitate before answering. "Nan...well, Nan is no longer with me."

"What?"

When he said nothing, I added, "I'm sorry, it's just...she seemed so devoted to you. Did she...did she leave because of the scandal?"

"No. She didn't leave. That is, she did, but because I decided to let her go."

"You fired her? Why?"

"Well," he said, clearly pained, "I wouldn't use the word 'fire.' The official story is that I realized I needed someone with a real estate license, and a friend of mine at the Lighthouse was prepared to offer her better compensation anyway."

"And the real story?"

"The real story is that she was a perfect assistant, and even in two lifetimes, I couldn't hope to find a better one. But—"

I could see how hard it was for him to go on.

"You don't have to tell me if you'd rather not," I said.

"No, it's okay. Where else would I have the luxury of iron-clad confidentiality?"

I smiled encouragingly, then realized he couldn't see this. I made myself murmur encouragingly instead.

"Look," he said, "as I'm sure you can imagine, the relationship with an assistant is an intimate one, and because I'm blind, it's especially so with me. What other married CEO would walk around in public, holding his assistant's arm? In hindsight, there was probably a little too much symbiosis there, but anyway. Without going into too much detail…well, she crossed a line. Nothing sexual happened, if that's how it sounds. No indiscretion in the usual sense. And at first, I thought I could get past it. But I couldn't. Maybe if all this other stuff weren't going on, it would have been different. But once that can of snakes was open, it just created this incredible tension. And there's so much other tension right now that any more is untenable."

"I understand," I said. "And I'm sorry."

We turned then to the matters at hand. I informed Abel that the issue of *predisposition* is often what makes or breaks an entrapment defense.

"We have to demonstrate that you had no predisposition to commit this crime. A while back, you mentioned returning Christmas gifts—even bottles of champagne—to corporate vendors, rather than risk the appearance of accepting a bribe. We need to compile a list of those vendors and explore their suitability as witnesses…"

After Abel left, I went back into my office and locked the door. I needed to finally call my sister back—in the face of my ongoing silence, her messages were becoming distraught—but I didn't want to speak to her from home, where Darren could overhear.

"I have to talk with you, Leda," I said the moment she picked up the phone.

There was a startled pause and then she sputtered in indignation. "Oh, and I haven't been around? I haven't taken your calls? Haven't returned them either? Did you leave a bunch of messages that no one could be bothered to answer?"

"All right, all right," I said. I was a little taken aback. "I'll admit I was very upset about something, and I needed some time before I could have a conversation."

"Upset about what?"

"Okay, listen." At the back of my desk drawer was a very old, very stale, nearly empty pack of cigarettes and now I fished one from the box and cracked open the window to smoke it. "Last time we talked? Remember I needed to check whether our passports were expired? Well, I went into Darren's file cabinet to look for them. And—well—I found a porn video."

"Oh for Christ's sake, Lily," Leda said after a long moment. "Is that what all this drama is about? Good God. Give the guy a break, would you? Unless it's little boys or something."

"It's not little boys," I said, and shut my eyes. "It's you."

It was barely audible, but I heard it: her quick intake of breath. A sound of surprise and distress. It was a long moment before she spoke.

"*Payback*? Is that what you're talking about?"

"Yes."

"Well. Lily. Look. I was really, really young," she said. She was very flustered. "I'm not sure who you're mad at, Darren or me. Knowing you, probably both of us. But it was a long time ago for me, it's ancient history. I was practically a kid. What do you care, anyway? What I do with my life is my business."

"Yeah, God forbid you should ever think about how something like that could affect me. Now that I think of it, with my high-profile cases, it's like a miracle that no tabloid has broken it out and speculated that it was me. But I'm sure that possibility never crossed your mind, since you don't tend to think much about anyone besides yourself."

"Yeah, I admit that wasn't my main concern when we were

nineteen and you weren't even in law school yet. Plus, I mean, I'm kind of incognito. It's not my real name—"

"Leda Swann?"

"—and I had a platinum dye-job. And blue contacts. I'd be shocked if anyone ever linked it to you. It would take someone who's known you from way back, someone who knows you really well."

"Why, yes," I said, "Like Darren, for instance, now that you mention it. I mean, maybe you can't appreciate this, but it *is* just a slight bit awkward knowing my husband's jerking off to my *sister's* porn performance."

"Well, I—I mean…that's not really my fault, Lily, Darren wasn't even in your life back then! And…and I get why Darren would buy something like that. I mean, come on, be fair. Imagine being in his place. It must have felt like seeing his wife on a porn store shelf. How could he *not*…I mean…how could he not at least *look*?"

"Well," I said, blowing smoke out the window, "he didn't just look. He bought the thing and hid it from me for who knows how many years. And how would he have found it in the first place if he wasn't already on some porn site?"

"Yeah, that's a great point. He went to a porn site! You'd better kick his ass to the curb along with the morning trash and every other man in the free world."

"Oh—right—all men do it, that's just the way they are, and we can't expect any better from them, and so on and so forth *ad nauseam.* But the point is, Darren doesn't just pretend to be above porn, he's always joined me in actively *condemning* it. Which makes him not just weak and sleazy, but a fraud. A hypocrite."

When Leda was silent, I continued, "But that doesn't really involve you. We can leave that between him and me. What I want you to tell me is: why *this* movie? I mean, okay, you're an exhibitionist and you want to fuck your boyfriend on camera and know that other people are paying to watch. Fine. But why does it have to be the most degrading story line imaginable?"

"Is that a serious question? Really? I mean, please. Who cares what the storyline was? If it didn't feel degrading to me, then why should you get bent out of shape about it?"

But before I had a chance to consider my answer to this, my sister suddenly said, "You know what I think?"

"What?"

"I mean, you want to know the real reason I think this is bothering you?"

I would not ask again. I would not be *baited*. I resolved to just wait her out. I didn't have to wait long.

"I bet it's because *you can't stand that it gets you fucking hot*."

I hung up the phone. I resisted—just barely—the urge to throw it across the room. I took a deep angry drag on my cigarette and put it out on the windowsill, taking satisfaction in the way it scarred the paint.

How dare she? The smug insinuating fucking bitch.

The red light flashed on my phone, which meant an incoming call was being held at the front desk. I grabbed the receiver and addressed the receptionist.

"Yes, Penny?"

"Your sister is on line one."

"Please take a message," I said, and hung up again.

I would not talk to her. I would not visit her. She and her husband could move by themselves. I'd let her twist in the wind a lot longer this time.

But even as I was thinking this, I could hear her voice in my mind yet again. *What's the matter? Truth hurt?*

I lit another cigarette, went back to the window.

Once, at a judge's retirement party, a drunk prosecutor—one

I'd opposed in court on several occasions—came up to me at the open bar and told me I was the queen of his hate-fuck fantasies. Even as I stepped away, repelled, his words were like a black-gloved hand between my legs and for months afterward, I replayed them in my mind whenever I needed inspiration with Darren. I'd lie in bed beneath my husband and think of the prosecutor's hard eyes and whiskey breath and loosened tie, the idea that he both hated and wanted me. The knowledge that he went home and thought of me while bringing himself off: who would believe how intoxicating I found it? I wasn't that kind of woman.

I left another cigarette scar on the sill, made myself return to my desk, spent the next few hours looking at the contents of my inbox without really taking any of it in. My concentration was shot.

Toward the end of the day, my paralegal came into my office with a sheet of paper.

"Kamin's office just sent this over," she said. "It's an updated witness list for the Nathanson case."

At first glance, it didn't look much different from the list we already had. And it wasn't. Only one witness had been added.

I didn't recognize the surname Magdalene.

But I knew the first name well.

Nan.

When I got home, Darren was at the dinner table by himself with a carton of lo mein and a bottle of Tsingtao.

"What's the story with you and Leda?" he asked before I'd closed the door behind me. "She called half an hour ago. She says you won't talk to her. She sounded very upset."

"Good," I said. "She should be upset." I hung my coat in the closet and stepped out of my shoes.

"Well, what's going on? She won't tell me."

"I'd really rather not tell you either. It's private." Hell would freeze over before I'd repeat what Leda had said to me.

"Fine. You don't have to tell me, but you should call her back. She was begging me to convince you, Lil."

"Begging. Now there's a trick," I said, going to the liquor cabinet. "Maybe she'll heel or fetch for you next."

My husband looked at me in bewilderment.

I grabbed a bottle of Bacardi and slammed the cabinet shut. "Isn't that what the two of you are into?"

"What in the name of Christ is the matter with you?"

Darren didn't get angry very often, but I could suddenly see that he was very angry now. And just as suddenly, I understood I had gone too far.

"Okay," I said. I took a deep breath, looking away from him. "Listen, I'm sorry. I had a real setback today at work."

I watched anger struggle with sympathy on his face. "What happened?"

I moved to the table and sat down next to him. "My client's former assistant—who might have provided invaluable testimony on his behalf if he hadn't *fired* her last week—showed up on the prosecution's witness list this afternoon," I said. "And there's no telling how much damage she'll do."

"That's not good," Darren conceded.

"He doesn't know yet. I asked him to come by tomorrow morning. I want to tell him in person."

"I'd do the same."

"But I can't tell you how I'm dreading it. I mean, it could easily be our undoing."

Darren put a hand on my shoulder and we sat there a moment. I felt a flash of the old closeness with him.

Then he said, "Listen, Lil. I don't want to be in the middle of whatever's going on with you and Leda. Of course you'll do as you decide. But I can't help hoping you'll reach out to her."

And my sense of connection with him vanished, just like that. I couldn't help but feel he was taking her side, pleading her case.

But I also couldn't dwell on that right now. I had to figure out how to tell my client that his former assistant would be testifying against him. I had to find a way to control whatever happened when she took the stand. I had to take her down, and I was going to need his help.

"Abel," I said the next morning, when he was seated in my office with his dog at his feet. "I have some bad news."

He tilted his head, waiting.

"The prosecution sent over an updated list of witnesses," I went on. "And your former assistant is on it."

"*Nan?*"

"I'm afraid so."

"No," he said. "I can't believe that."

"Well," I said carefully, "they would have been remiss not to question her. Any ex-employee, especially one you recently let go, would be likely to yield something of use."

He passed a hand over his face. For a moment, I was afraid he might cry.

"Well, but what damage can she really do?" he asked after a long moment. "I'm not denying the misappropriation of funds."

"It depends on how bitter she is, how vindictive she might be feeling," I said. "She could testify, for example, that she overheard your conversation with Tom Roscoe, and that letting the city underwrite your sister's repairs was your idea, not his. Is she angry enough to lie on the stand? Because Roscoe will certainly say the idea was yours, and if she were disputing that, her name wouldn't be on their witness list."

I paused to let this sink in.

"Beyond that," I went on, "she could also testify as a character witness. She could tell the jury you're a greedy, lying, conniving bastard."

"Jesus Christ," he said. "Let me contact her."

"No," I told him. "You can't. She's with them now. They might be recording all her calls, anticipating a conversation like the one you want to have with her. At the very least, we have to assume she would testify about such a phone call. Any appearance on your part of trying to sway her testimony would be catastrophic."

He sat back in his seat, defeated.

"I shouldn't have let her go," he said after a while. "I handled it all wrong."

"Why *did* you let her go? I mean, you told me she crossed a line, but you didn't say how. It didn't matter then, but now it does. You need to tell me what happened."

"It's hard to explain."

I waited.

"She had an unnerving past," he said eventually.

"Something that could discredit her as a witness?"

"Oh God," he said. "I don't want to go there."

"What? Why the hell not?"

"She was so devoted to me."

"And now she may well be just as devoted to destroying you."

"That's not fair," he said. He was very distraught. "It's not fair to her. Why should she have to pay for my mistakes?"

"Abel," I said. "Do you want Lulu to have a father in prison?"

He sat there in agony.

"Listen," I said after a long moment, softening my tone. "I need to understand what we're dealing with here. I can't get at Nan's motives or her state of mind or her weaknesses as an adversary without information. To have any hope of neutralizing her testimony, I need to know everything about her that you can tell me."

"She worked for a place called the Nutcracker Suite," he said finally. "It was a place where people pay to engage in S&M."

I went still, staring at the ruled yellow paper of my legal tablet. Here it was. Confirmation of something I'd felt all along.

And then, just as quickly, this dark thrill of recognition was displaced by professional assessment. My personal response had no place here. This kind of compartmentalization was as natural to me as breathing.

"Ah," I said. I looked up at him. "This is good for us. So she tied men up and whipped them? Stuff like that?"

"No, she played the slave. Presumably men tied her up and whipped her."

And here I felt the first surge of optimism since seeing Nan's name on the witness list. "Well. That is good news—very good news. You do realize this is priceless for the defense? I mean, a job like that would discredit any witness. Frankly, for most jurors I think it will call her sanity into question."

He went silent again and I realized I could not let myself gloat over her undoing. Not out loud. Not to him.

"Look, I'm sorry," I said. "I understand that you have some …residual sympathy for her, and I don't doubt that you have good reasons. I mean, she sounds like a troubled person. Do you have any sense of what drew her to that line of work?"

"I never asked her," he said.

"Really? In more than two years of—as you put it—a very intimate relationship?"

"It was intimate," he said, "but it was still very much a formal working relationship, and to be honest, a lot of that formality came from her.

"It's not that I ever forgot about her past. You don't forget something like that. And just between you and me, I should acknowledge that there was something between us, something we never talked about. As I've said before, nothing sexual happened with her, and in fact I don't think she even *wanted* anything sexual to happen. But she took pleasure in serving me. I knew that. And look, I'll admit that I liked it. I mean, Christ, who wouldn't? She would have done anything for me. And so our interests were perfectly aligned. She didn't hope to be promoted. Didn't want to learn the business, climb the company ladder, advance her career.

"She wanted a place where there was no room to move," he concluded. "I gave it to her."

As soon as Abel was gone, the call button on my phone began to flash and I let Penny put Leda through. Not because I was ready to forgive her, but because I realized that the angrier I seemed about what she had said, the more implicit validation I was giving it.

"Lily," she said. "I'm so glad you took my call."

"Well, don't be, not yet," I said. "I'm still angry. But not for the reason you think."

"Well, why then?"

"I don't care what misguided ideas you have about what turns me on," I told her. "But I still can't believe you never told me about that movie. That in all these years, you never said one word."

"Oh come on, Lily, how could I? You know how you are."

"No, I don't. How am I?"

"You're a great lawyer," she said, "and someday you'll probably be a judge. And you should be. Because at the end of the day, that's what you are. All right?"

It stung. I felt my throat close over, and I didn't answer.

"And that's why *I'm* angry at *you*. I hate that you called Darren a fraud and a hypocrite. You have no idea how lucky you are.

You think it's easy to find guys like him? Smart and supportive and loyal? Not to mention handsome as hell."

"Well, you two are quite the mutual admiration society," I managed to say. I heard the way I sounded: catty and jealous. "And apparently hot for each other to boot. Maybe *you* should have married him."

My husband's words of the other night came back to me: *What in the name of Christ is the matter with you?* I didn't know. I had a sudden urge to cry.

There was a long silence, maybe a whole minute. But when Leda finally broke it, her voice had gone soft and wistful.

"Oh, Lily. You know what I'm thinking of right now? Lily, are you there? Remember when you first stopped eating meat? You probably don't remember this, but you and Darren and I, we were out somewhere for Mexican and you were totally miserable. You couldn't have a single thing you wanted. It was just starting to dawn on you how many different things you liked that you could never have again. You were going to get the lentil soup or something, but you were bummed.

"Darren asked you what was wrong. You sat there staring at the menu and you didn't answer. So I told him you wanted the steak fajitas. And do you remember what he said then?"

I sat waiting to hear. Leda continued.

"He said, *You can, you know.* He was looking at you with so much love. I was so jealous of you right then. I wanted a man to look at me that way. Do you remember, Lil?"

But suddenly I didn't trust myself to speak.

After a moment, Leda went on. "He said: *You can have them. I won't tell anyone.*"

When I hung up the phone, I was no longer angry, just bewildered and sad. When had I become this version of myself? But as usual, I didn't have time to think about it. I turned my attention to the task at hand: finding out exactly what went on at the Nutcracker Suite.

As I was leaving the office that evening, Penny hailed me from the reception desk. A few hours before, I'd asked her to clear my schedule for the next morning. I said something unexpected had come up and apologized for the short notice.

"I've canceled your 10:00 A.M. meeting with Tam MacNamara," she said. "But she's out of town next week, so she—"

Just then the UPS man buzzed and I told her I'd wait. As she went to meet him at the door and sign for whatever had arrived, my glance went to her desk, where a paperback copy of *The Maltese Falcon* had been laid face down, open to the page she was on. There was something odd about the cover, and after a moment I realized it had been ripped from another book and scotch-taped in place. The back cover was intact, and before Penny returned, I was able to read a fragment of the copy. *Prince Alejandro Del Castillo is used to taking what he wants…and he's determined that his lovely chambermaid will be no exception!*

8

The Nutcracker Suite was a surprise. It was more upscale than anything I'd pictured. Expensive leather furniture in the windowless waiting room, a mahogany executive-style desk in the reception area. I didn't see the other rooms right away. The madam of the place, Mistress DeVille, interviewed me in the kitchen, which was clean and well-lit. The fridge was stocked with bottled water and on the counter was coffee, tea and a jar of red licorice.

The mistress herself was tall and lean, with high cheekbones and fiery hair. I thought she was probably in her early forties. She wore a black latex jumpsuit with thigh-high black boots, but her manner was brisk and friendly.

Setting up this meeting had not been hard. When I'd called the day before, during regular business hours, the boss herself had answered the phone.

"Nutcracker Suite, Mistress DeVille speaking."

"I'm looking for work as a professional submissive," I told her, "and I wondered if you were hiring." I figured they had to be. I could not imagine that professional submissives were easy to find.

"We're always looking for special girls," Mistress DeVille confirmed. "What's your name, dear?"

"Leda," I told her.

"Leda, do you have any experience?"

"Oh, well, just—just what I've done with my boyfriend. That is, my ex-boyfriend," I improvised. "But he told me I was a natural."

"Well, a good attitude and an open mind are what matter the

most," she said. "Do you want to drop by tomorrow morning and learn more about the position? Then you can figure out whether it might be for you."

Why was I doing this? I needed to gather the specifics of what Nan had done for a living—the worse, the better. I needed to make her seem alien and disturbing to the jury. *Here, good ladies and gentlemen, is someone outside the bounds of decency, credibility and common sense.* Still, I could've had our private investigator get the scope of what went on there. Abel's retainer would have covered it.

But I told myself it was better if I went. I needed a visceral and immediate sense of the place, the better to glean the stray and unexpected details that were often the most effective.

In trying to look the part of a hopeful applicant, I dispensed with my usual chignon, traded my glasses for contacts, and even put on a little makeup. I wore an old plaid skirt I'd had since college and the closest thing I had to a low-cut blouse. I felt so different in this attire: girlish and strangely vulnerable, as if I really did want this job, and was both excited and frightened by the prospect of getting it.

"How old are you, dear?" Mistress Deville asked me in the Nutcracker kitchen.

"Twenty-nine." I looked young for thirty-six, everyone said so.

"Well, you're very pretty. And the fact that you're a little older is actually a good thing, believe it or not. I'm just not comfortable hiring very young girls. I think this job requires some maturity. Now, Leda, there's a list of activities that our dominant clients may choose to engage in. You need to be willing to participate in most if not all of them. I'm going to go through them one by one and I advise you to be completely honest about what you will and won't do. If you misrepresent yourself, it'll just be a waste of everyone's time. Am I clear?

"Yes."

"Okay. Over-the-knee spanking?"

"Yes."

I had resolved ahead of time to say yes to everything. Otherwise, how would I get to hear all that went on there?

"Corner time? This might involve kneeling for up to an hour."

"Yes."

"Mouth-soaping?"

Ugh. "Yes."

"Role-playing. This might mean being daddy's little brat, or a naughty schoolgirl, or a careless secretary, and so on."

"I'm fine with all of that."

"Golden showers?"

"Well…I guess so. Yes."

Even as I winced inwardly with every checklist item, I was thrilled by the acts I'd be able to pin on Nan.

"All right, Leda, now I'm going to name some implements our clients might want to use in a session. You tell me whether you think you could handle it."

"Okay."

"Do you know what a flogger is? It's like a cat-o-nine-tails. A lot of leather strands. Ever felt one?"

"Yes. I like those."

"What about a riding crop?"

"That's fine. Yes."

"Paddles?"

"Yes."

"Canes?"

"Yes."

And on it went: a dizzying list of tortures and indignities, to which I said yes, and yes, and yes again. And as I sat there imagining these acts and offering my compliance with every one of them, I had the strange sense that I'd opened a window and crawled through it into another realm, another life, one in which erotic desire assumed an unapologetic primacy. It was strangely disconcerting, disorienting.

Here it is, I thought, though I wasn't sure what "it" was. *Here I am*. Whatever else it was, it was a place I'd never been.

"Well," Mistress Deville said after I'd expressed a willingness to take three strokes—the maximum number allowed within a single session—with a single-tail bullwhip. "I'm impressed. For someone who's only dabbled with her boyfriend, you seem up for anything."

"Well, um…he was kind of hard-core, actually," I said.

"Apparently." She made a note on her paper. "Are you willing to be bound and gagged?"

I decided to show a little last-minute skittishness, if only to lend my performance credibility.

"Well…I would be, if…um, can I ask a question?"

"Of course."

"Do you do anything to make sure the…girls…are safe in a session?" It killed me to say *girls* instead of *women*.

"I'm very glad you asked that. Of course we do. The clients don't know this, and I'm telling you in the strictest confidence, but we have cameras in the rooms and someone is watching each session at all times."

"I don't mind being tied up if that kind of protection is in place."

"Also, before each session begins, you and the client will decide on a safe word for you to use if need be. Did you and your boyfriend use a safe word?"

"A safe word? No, we didn't."

"Well, a safe word solves the problem of how the dominant is to know when a submissive has reached a genuine limit. It lets you beg and moan in character without stopping the action.

So for instance, let's say your safe word is *mercy*. You can whimper and plead, in keeping with your role, for the client to stop doing whatever he's doing to you, and he can pretend to ignore your wishes. But if you say *mercy*, he knows you truly want or need him to stop. And our rules demand that he do so. If he doesn't, we will stop the session and throw him out of here, and he won't ever be allowed back in."

I nodded as if I were glad to know this.

"So. Now that you know a little about what we do, would you like a tour of the place?"

She led me through a series of rooms, beginning with a vast space washed in crimson light. This was the main 'dungeon,' with two cages, both large enough to accommodate a man. One was on the floor, the other suspended by a chain from the ceiling. There was a St. Catherine's Wheel, an upright structure on which submissives could be bound and spun; a St. Andrew's Cross, which seemed to serve as a whipping post; a sling, a stockade, and an entire wall hung with whips and paddles and canes.

"Have you ever suffered from claustrophobia?" Mistress Deville tossed over her shoulder, seemingly as an afterthought. "Any issues with being locked in a cage?"

"No."

There was a medical room with an examination table, a cabinet stocked with first aid supplies, a row of metal devices laid out on a Formica countertop: syringes and forceps and speculums. Everything was white or gleaming silver: cold and sterile and merciless.

There was a classroom with a blackboard and rows of chairs with built-in desks. There was a pointer and yardstick and a dunce cap hanging from a peg in the corner.

There was a soundproofed room for sensory deprivation, with

leather cuffs dangling from each corner of a padded restraint table.

The smallest room was just a jail cell with a walkway in front of it, and a closet full of guard uniforms, handcuffs and shackles.

It was impossible to walk through these rooms without feeling twinges of what they were meant to arouse: fear, dread, fascination, nostalgia. It was impossible not to think of the scenes that had played out here. The overriding aromas of disinfectant and leather couldn't fully mask the more pungent ones just beneath: the musk of sweat, the gamy tang of struggle and tension and intensity.

When we were back in the kitchen, she said, "Do you have any other questions?"

"Well," I said, trying to imagine what I would ask if I were truly interested in the job. "I'm wondering what the pay is like."

She peered at me for a long moment and I had the uncomfortable sense that she was really seeing me for the first time. I made myself hold her gaze until one corner of her mouth went up and she shook her head ever so slightly.

"Something tells me we won't need to go into that. The money is quite decent, but—regardless of your financial situation—that's not your main motivation, is it? No. If it were just about money, no one would do it. You'd be looking for work as a domme if that was what you were after. Professional subs are here because they need what goes on within these walls.

"Now, I own this place. I run it. Do you know what it takes to make it as far as I have in this business? Intuition. Radar. The ability to read people. I have that. And do you want to know what my intuition is telling me right now?"

I looked at her in alarm. She didn't wait for me to speak.

"You're not seriously thinking of working here. Whatever your need is, you're not going to satisfy it here and you know that. You're too controlling to surrender to total strangers, men you've never met.

"And that's too bad, for us at least. Because your boyfriend was right: you are a natural. You do genuinely yearn to submit; I can see that."

My face became so hot that I could feel the blood pounding beneath my cheekbones and it actually hurt.

"You're embarrassed. Why?"

"Well, I…because…" I stuttered. "Because you're probably right, I mean…this seems like a great place, but what you said about strangers and needing control and all that…I think it might be true. That I'm not ready to be a pro. And I—I feel bad about taking your time."

"Oh, don't give it another thought," she said. "It's a slow morning and I like you. And maybe, given time, you'll feel differently. If and when that day arrives, we'll be here. You can count on that."

And a few moments later, as I stepped through the heavy door and into the corridor, she said, "Good luck, dear."

Remembering all this now, in the tavern, a question came to me, one I hadn't planned to ask.

"Abel told me about the Nutcracker Suite, and your position there," I told Nan. I didn't mention I had visited the place myself. "And he said he never asked you this, but I will: what was it like?"

9

Nan's name at the Nutcracker was O, after the most famous slave in literature, and she found the initial fitting. O, after all, was for open, for offering and obliging, for obedient and obsequious, for Ophelia and odalisque. O was for order and ordeal, for overtaken and owned. For outcry and orgasm and obsession. For orphan. And like O herself, Nan held her body in a certain way whenever a man stood in the doorway looking them over. She never crossed or closed her legs, never even allowed her knees to touch. Her lips, too, were always slightly apart. She would raise her gaze to the man's for the briefest moment, then lower her eyes for the duration of his decision. To smile at him or to speak first would have been unthinkable.

She was an unusual submissive by anyone's standards. Many of the regular clients never once contracted for her, preferring the lighthearted, the childish, the coy or sexually overt. But the ones who did choose her tended to be what she wanted: serious, deliberate, devoted to form, desirous of a regular liaison. Many of them arranged to see her outside the establishment, where they initiated her into their ongoing service.

One of these men, for instance, insisted that she call him at ten o'clock every night. He would accept no reason for her failure to do so. He had a special phone line for this purpose alone, with an answering machine that would record the time of her call in his absence. The hour had to be precisely ten, not a minute before or after. Nan learned not to see a nine o'clock movie, lest she lose several minutes of the film to a payphone in the lobby. She learned never to book an evening flight, nor to go to bed early without setting an alarm, nor to accept a dinner date after eight o'clock. If she were on the subway, she would have to get off the train at 9:50 wherever she happened to be, find a phone in the station, or go up to the street before paying the fare again.

On the rare occasions that Nan was a minute or so off, his retribution during the following session was merciless. Once she was on a train that stopped between stations for half an hour. She pleaded with him to take this into account, but he wouldn't hear of it.

"You should consider every possibility before putting yourself into a situation you can't control," he told her. "You'd leave yourself an extra hour to get to the airport—wouldn't you?—if you had an urgent destination and a non-refundable ticket. Because if something went wrong, all the good reasons in the world wouldn't keep you from missing that flight. It wouldn't matter that it wasn't your fault, that you couldn't get a cab during rush hour, that the main roads were closed or that there was a five-mile gridlock. Your plane would be gone.

"I'm sure you play it safe whenever you travel," he continued. "Your commitment to me should call for the same consideration and forethought. In fact, it should call for more."

He punctuated this lecture with ten searing stripes of a rattan cane, and when it was over she went to her knees and, still weeping, kissed the full length of it as he drew it across her lips. She loved this man. She loved having some version of a curfew. She slept better, within the inflexibility of his rule, than ever before or since, until she began working for Abel. She was bereft when he accepted a job offer in Hong Kong.

Another man would not allow her to say the word "no" in his presence. This went beyond expressions of refusal or defiance to include any use of the word. She couldn't say *Oh no* or *No problem* or *I have no idea*.

"Sir, may I ask a question?"

"You may."

"Sir, if I'm not using…*that word*…to defy an order or oppose you in any way, then what is the purpose of this rule?"

"Its purpose," he said, "is that it will force you, always, to think before you speak to me."

And it did; in mid-sentence, Nan often had to stop and rephrase what she was about to say.

"What's the chance of having you accompany me on a business trip next week?" he asked on one occasion. This was in the lounge of the Paramount Hotel, where he liked to have a late-night drink.

"Sir, I'm afraid there's…that there isn't any chance, unless one of the other girls is willing to work double shifts every day I'm gone."

"Well, don't you get vacation time?"

"Sir, I'm afraid I don't."

"Miss," the hostess hailed her on her way back from the ladies' room. "Would you please tell your companion there's no smoking in the lounge?"

"Sir," she said, when she returned to the table. "The hostess has asked me to tell you that smoking isn't permitted in the lounge."

And then there was the man who didn't believe in bondage. He considered the very idea of it an affront to his authority. "If I tell you to assume a certain position," he told her, "and to hold that position until I give you permission to break it, then you're not going to move. If I have to resort to physical restraint—if I need cuffs or chains to keep you in place—then there's something wrong with the way I've trained you."

It felt so strange afterward to be given tips. The man transformed, his pretend rage dissipated. No, not pretend, it was never pretend, but it was no longer apparent or accessible. He would be kindly, distracted, in a hurry.

Out on the street again, Nan would walk gingerly, her body welted and tender beneath the hooded jackets and sweatpants she always brought along to wear home. She often felt hollow, transcendent, as if she were pure spirit and the pain was what weighed her to the earth. Other times, in a way that made no sense even to her, she felt hurt and close to tears. She felt pangs of aftershock, arousal, and bewildered grief all at the same time.

The world outside was always jarring, with its noise and neon, its crowded sidewalks. Making her way home after a heavy scene, the text of the session written into her body, she kept her arms and legs covered even in the summer. If the encounter was a good one, she would stand naked before her full-length mirror, survey the marks on her body with a kind of pride, and savor the sight of them over the next several days. If it was bad, she would hide the bruises even from herself.

Her favorite part of the job was her occasional trips to other cities to visit wealthy men well known to the establishment. It was at these times that she felt most free: moving through foreign airports toward the homes of strangers, where her job would be to endure whatever they brought down upon her. To stand trembling, waiting. To suffer and to beg. She used to dream that she would find her true place in one of these houses. But she always knew within minutes that she would be turning around and coming back.

The opposite happened the day of her interview with Abel. Then she could see that the little room just off his office was where she belonged: underground and spare, threadbare and sad, two floors below his bed, and her covetous heart hurt with wanting it.

10

In the warm May air outside the Nutcracker, I felt out of sorts. With my girlish skirt and blouse, my hair long and loose, I had the strange sensation that I'd become someone else. And I didn't want that to end, at least not yet.

It was noon. I knew I should go back to work. But I found my thoughts drifting to a cocktail party being held that night at the midtown Hilton, hosted by the New York Bar Association in honor of some anniversary or other. It was the kind of event reliably attended by that prosecutor, the one whose drunken words I'd been thinking about with alarming frequency.

I didn't blame him for hating me; I'd earned it and in fact, I took a kind of pride in it. We'd been opponents in three different trials during the past decade and I'd burned him in each one: shredding his witnesses, raising relentless (and sustained) objections to his questions, even laughing in his face on one occasion when he offered my client a plea deal.

An outrageous idea came to me as I walked along, one I knew that I would not, could not, act upon—so why did it leave me in a cold and speculative sweat? I turned the corner and there in front of me was Saks Fifth Avenue.

I couldn't. I wouldn't. And yet. It was as if Leda's movie and the story about Nan and the visit to the Nutcracker had all unhinged me. Made me long for a secret life, a secret self, an hour or two in some flickering chamber beyond a threshold I had never crossed.

I found myself calling Penny. "Please clear my schedule for the rest of the day," I told her. "I thought I'd be able to come in this afternoon, but it turns out that I can't." Next I called my husband and spoke with him about the party, made sure he knew it would be a late night.

And then I went into Saks and bought a daring new blouse, lovely pale blue silk with a plunging neckline. I bought a black silk skirt, its hemline higher than anything I'd ever owned. I bought a black pair of stiletto pumps with five-inch heels, a black g-string and garter belt and thigh-high stockings. I went home—it was the middle of the afternoon—and soaked in the tub with sweet almond oil and tried to steady my own breathing.

Some time later I drew on my new lingerie, then my new blouse and skirt. I stepped into the ludicrous shoes and pressed perfume behind my ears. I pinned my hair up with little jeweled clips, pulling a stray strand or two loose on each side. I put on mascara and lipstick and diamond earrings.

Then I went out to hail a cab instead of walking to the subway. And in the lobby of the Hilton, in the mirror above the courtesy phones, I barely recognized myself.

The party was on the mezzanine level and I saw him as soon as I walked into the room. He was standing by the fireplace, a drink in his hand, talking to an older judge.

At the bar, I knocked back two margaritas, tracking him with what I hoped were subtle sidelong glances. When the judge drifted away, I stood immediately and crossed the room, clutching my third drink for nerve.

When I was before him, I spoke without preamble. "Do you remember what you said to me the last time we were at one of these things?"

Fortunately he seemed to have had a few himself. He regarded me with interest. "I have a feeling you're about to refresh my memory."

"You told me I was the queen of your hate-fuck fantasies. You said, *Oh, what I've dreamed of doing to you.*"

He showed not a hint of chagrin. "Did I say that? Well, you can't blame a guy for dreaming, can you?"

"What if I offered you the chance to do more than dream?"

He tilted his head to one side and narrowed his eyes. "You can't possibly be propositioning me," he said. "Can you?"

I drained my glass and handed it to him. "I'm going back to the bar. You're going to follow me and buy my fourth drink. While I'm having that, you're going to go down to the front desk and get a room. Then you'll come back, tell me the room number, slide one of the keys under my cocktail napkin, and go upstairs first. I'll join you there within ten minutes.

"Once I'm in the room, you'll call the shots. You'll have your way with me. You can do everything you've dreamed of and then some. That is, unless you don't have the balls."

I turned and went back to the bar. I didn't look behind me; I didn't look around. I pretended to check my phone for messages. A moment later, I felt him beside me.

He tossed a ten-dollar bill onto the bar. "Give the girl whatever she wants," he told the bartender. And then he was gone.

Girl.

I sat still and sipped the lovely cold drink, hardly believing this. There was a delicious haze to everything. I felt impossibly sexy. Like a sassy, brassy, bossy lady about to get her cum-uppance.

And then he was beside me again, leaning in, speaking low. "Room 1108," he said. And he slid the key card beneath my napkin before moving away.

I didn't touch it. I sat there. I drank. Everything was electric. Was this what Leda's life was like? Had she had these adventures throughout her youth? There were several men already in the elevator when I stepped in and pressed the button for the eleventh floor. They stared at me. I'd always considered myself reasonably attractive to men, but they had never stared at me, not like this. Something was coming off me like heat, something they felt. No one spoke. They were mute with longing and frustration, there in the close confines of the elevator. And I loved it.

I stood in front of room 1108 for a long moment before pushing my key card into its slot and nudging the door open. He was across the room, in one of two chairs flanking a table by the window. He had come straight from work like everyone but me, and he'd retrieved his briefcase from the coat check. It was at his feet and he had papers on the table, papers in which he was feigning interest.

"May I come in?" I asked.

"Come in and close the door behind you and then stay just where you are," he said. "And from this point on, you'll address me as sir."

"Yes, sir," I said, and waited for further direction.

"Take off your blouse and hang it in the closet to your left."

I held his gaze as I unfastened every button on my blouse. I hung it up and then, in response to his gesture, took off my bra as well and draped it over the same hanger.

"Now lean against the door, facing me," he said. "Put your hands above your head, your palms against the wall."

Alcohol had slowed my comprehension and it took a moment to make sense of these instructions, but once I had, I obeyed.

"Good. Now stay just like that," he told me, and resumed his perusal of the papers on the table.

I stood there, waiting. Arousal broke over me like a wave and I closed my eyes.

"Look at me," he said sharply, and I opened them again.

For the next while—how long? Ten minutes, twenty?—he

made a show of going through the contents of his briefcase. I had time to take in every detail of the room—the black-and-white photo of the New York City skyline above the headboard, the heavy mauve curtains and the sheer white scrim behind them, the sparkling view through the window, the wide expanse of the bed.

I had time to take in every detail of him. He was handsome. His tie was loosened. His shoes were shined.

By the time he put his papers aside, my scant black panties were soaked through and there was an ache between my legs.

Finally he stood and slowly approached me until we were eye to eye. He had a few inches on me but not many. Looking straight into my gaze, he took off his belt and held it across my mouth.

"Kiss it," he said.

I kissed it.

"Kiss it like you'd like to kiss me," he said. "Kiss it like you love it."

My mouth opened and I tongued the leather, nipped at it like a kitten.

He took it away and cracked it against the wall next to my head. I whimpered in real fear. Then he wrapped it around my neck, sliding the leather end through the buckle so that it was at once a collar and a leash.

"Down on all fours," he said.

I dropped to the carpet and let him lead me—him walking, me crawling—to the foot of the bed.

"We're going to play a little game," he said. "As much as I intend to enjoy my complete power over you this evening, I'm feeling generous enough to grant you a way of expressing a preference. If I give you an order or undertake some action you truly wish to escape, you may impart your protest with a single word. What do you think that word should be?"

I understood what he was doing. It was what Mistress DeVille had described just that morning. He was giving me a safe word.

"I—I haven't given any thought to that, sir."

"Of course you haven't. So think about it now. And be quick about it."

"What about...*mercy*?"

" 'Mercy.' I like the sound of that. I'd like to hear you beg for mercy, and I promise that you will, but no, that won't be your word. I've just thought of a better one, a word you take every opportunity to use as it is—one you never hesitate to invoke with all the passion you've reserved for such endeavors up until now. And so it will be a special ironic pleasure to hear it in this context. If you'd like me to reconsider something on my agenda, you'll say *objection*."

I closed my eyes, strangely humiliated.

"Is that understood?"

"Yes, sir."

He tugged me to my feet and indicated that I should mount the lower left corner of the bed. "Stay on your hands and knees," he said, and I positioned myself in this way, facing the head-board but directly in front of him. I was still fully clothed from the waist down, including spike heels. He lifted the hem of my skirt and draped it across the small of my back, baring my ass.

Then I felt his hands at the back of my neck. My makeshift collar slackened and he took it off, then snapped it in the air, so close to my backside that I could feel the little current of air it left in its wake. I yelped in fear.

His hand on me, then. Moving his palm in slow circles against my right ass cheek.

"Has anyone ever beaten this beautiful ass?" he asked.

"No, sir."

"No? That's a shame and a mistake. Your husband doesn't keep you in line that way? Not ever?"

"No sir," I said again.

"Then he's a fool. Maybe next time he'll join us and I'll show him how it's done. But first I'm going to show you." He doubled the belt and brought it into my peripheral vision so I could see him gripping it by the buckle and opposite end. "First I'm going to give you a good working over with this belt of mine. What do you say to that?"

"Objection!"

He laughed, moved around the corner of the bed so he was alongside me, and closed a fist around my hair.

"Overruled," he said, and brought the doubled leather down hard.

No one had ever struck me in my life. It was a shock: the bite of the leather, the searing stripe it left across that vulnerable area where lower ass meets upper thigh. I cried out in pain and surprise.

He spoke low against my ear. "When I strike you, I expect you to thank me."

"Thank you, sir!" I said through gritted teeth.

So. Not a safe word after all. Which meant I didn't have one.

He struck me again, and again I cried out. But this time he didn't have to prompt me. "Thank you, sir!"

And on it went. The belt came down again and again, the blows raining all over my backside and thighs, punctuated by my expressions of gratitude and, yes—as he had promised—my pleas for mercy. And yet even as I whimpered and howled and wept and begged, there was a heat rising in me like the heat of the tequila I'd had earlier, warming me from within, and never in my life had I been more turned on. I could not believe any of this. Couldn't believe a man was *giving me a whipping*, that I was presenting myself for it, holding still for it, letting myself be punished and humbled.

"You think you're so tough," he said. "You're not so tough now, are you?" The belt cracked down across the back of my legs.

"Ahh! No, sir!"

"You think you're so *superior*. You've always looked at me like I'm not good enough to shine your shoes. Those days are over, though. I guarantee this evening will leave you with an attitude adjustment. Instill a little respect. Teach you some manners."

Every once in a while, he held the doubled leather in front of my mouth and I kissed it hungrily, as if its violence might be stayed with a show of passion.

"I want you to apologize for the way you've treated me in the past," he said, lashing me for emphasis.

"I'm sorry, sir!"

"I want you to beg for my forgiveness."

"I beg you to forgive me, sir!"

"Why are you such an ice-queen, Lillian?"

"I don't know, sir." My voice cracked, saying this.

"You're so cold. It's unbelievable to see you get hot. I never dreamed I'd see the day you'd be moaning and panting like a bitch in heat. This is better than anything I pictured." He wrapped his hand around my hair and tugged at it while he talked. "When you walk back into that courtroom, you're going to be different now, aren't you?"

"Yes, sir."

"The next time you're crucifying a witness of mine...or a judge sustains your objection to something I've said...or you hold a press conference to gloat over an acquittal...in the midst of every victory you ever have again, you're going to remember this. Aren't you?"

"Yes, sir," I said.

"Don't get me wrong. I know you'll do your job the way you always have, that you'll fight for your clients—but you're never going to look at me the same way again. Will you?"

"I—I don't expect so. Sir."

"No. I can promise you won't. Because I own you now. You understand that, right? It doesn't matter whether or not we ever meet like this again. This night happened and nothing you do or say will ever be able to change that. I've beaten your ass and made you cry and listened to you beg. I've made you howl, made you crawl, made you *apologize*."

He released my hair and brought his hand between my legs, penetrating me with two of his fingertips. I was very wet.

"And now I'm going to fuck you."

He paused as if to see whether the word *objection* would be forthcoming. It wasn't. I had learned that it was useless as a safe word but more to the point, I had no objection whatsoever.

"Kneel up and take off your skirt," he said, and I did so, unfastening the inner clasp and letting it fall, then returning to my hands and knees while he tugged it—and then my g-string— off me. I still wore my garter belt, thigh-high stockings and spike heels.

He hadn't removed a stitch of his own clothing but now he unzipped his fly and brought his cock through the opening of his trousers.

I felt just the tip of it penetrate me, no more than an inch deep.

"Imagine passing me in the courthouse halls a month from now," he continued. "Really think about it. Are you going to be able to look me in the eye?"

"I—I don't—"

"I can't wait to find out. I look forward to watching you in action and remembering this and knowing that you're remembering too. You'll always be naked in my presence now, no matter what kind of expensive threads you've got on. Do you know that?"

"Yes, sir…"

"You'll always be my bitch. Isn't that right?"

"Yes, sir."

"Say it. Tell me you'll always be my bitch."

"I'll always be your bitch, sir."

He was moving in and out of me ever so slightly, until I was so desperate for deeper penetration that I tried to back up onto his cock. He held me by the hips so I could go nowhere. I whimpered.

And then without warning he drove all the way into me. I cried out with pleasure but then he withdrew again, leaving just the tip inside me as before. I heard myself make a choking sound, as if swallowing a sob.

He repeated these intermittent thrusts a few more times—filling me delectably, pulling almost all the way out—until I was beside myself, barely aware of what I was saying.

Please sir please fuck me please give it to me I need it I beg you I'll do anything oh please sir oh please…

And suddenly he was pounding me with the intensity of a piston and it was all I could do just to hold still and take it. I lowered my head and grasped at the bedspread with both fists, trying to steady myself against the assault. It hurt but that didn't seem important and I closed my eyes and gave myself over to him as a stream of exciting words came to me, all those violent porn words, all those bodice-ripper words. *Nailed*, I thought. *Banged. Reamed, rammed, slammed. Riven* and *ravished* and *impaled. Overtaken*, I thought. *Taken over.*

I was moaning steadily and through this I was dimly aware

that his breathing had changed, that it had gone ragged and he was nearing the edge of his own release. And then there was a long, drawn-out groan as he spent himself.

In the stillness that followed, he stayed inside me. For long moments he stayed there, his hands still on my hips, and then his left palm drifted to caress the welts he'd left all over my backside. At the tenderness of this gesture, tears leaked silently from my eyes, staining the bedspread a darker blue.

Finally he eased himself out of me, and pulled back the bedcovers, and motioned me beneath them. I kicked my shoes off and crawled to the place he'd made for me. Then he stretched out beside me and pulled me close, drew my head down against his chest.

"That," he said, "was the best."

I looked up at him and smiled, almost too spent for words.

"I mean," he repeated. "That—was the very best—it has ever been."

"Yes," I said. "Yes. For me too, Darren."

"So," Nan said now, smiling faintly. "You worked out how the scene would go ahead of time?"

"Not the whole scene. Just the premise. On the phone that afternoon, I told Darren what the prosecutor had said years before, told him I wanted to act out his hate-fuck fantasy. He agreed to meet me at the party, already in character. But I didn't know how it would play out. I left the details to him."

"So he rose to the occasion."

"And how."

There was an awkward pause while I wavered over whether to say more. But then, why the hell not? I'd told her so much—too much—already.

"When Abel described your former job to me," I said, "I

couldn't stop thinking about it. I mean, it captured my imagination. It made me want to find out more. And...well, it helped me."

"I'm glad," she said.

I sat looking at her. Who knew what she was thinking? I had the feeling she saw me as an amateur, in every way. And after Abel's trial, I could hardly blame her. It pained me to remember it, and I knew it always would.

11

Abel's trial began on a bright clear morning. I'd been up since 5:00 A.M.—there was nothing like the excitement of a trial—and yet I felt full of energy and an almost predatory joy. It was game day.

Abel sat beside me at the defense table, his dog at his feet and his wife in the front row behind us. He was very pale but composed and stoic. As always, I was reminded of the disparity in what was at stake here for each of us. I fervently wanted to win each trial, for myself as well as for my client. My name and reputation—and some measure of my livelihood—was on the line. But it was nothing compared to what was at stake for Abel. If we lost, he could go to prison.

I wondered how it felt to sit in a courtroom without being able to see the judge, or the jury selected just yesterday, the seven men and five women who would decide his fate. With no way to read their faces, no way to gauge the way things were going.

We heard the knock of the judge and the bailiff called out. *All rise. Oyez, oyez, oyez. This court of the city of New York is now in session, the honorable Kendra Jenner presiding. Please be seated.*

I felt somewhat lucky that we had drawn Judge Jenner: a careful, thoughtful woman not given to gratuitous displays of power. She took her seat at the highest part of the room and issued the standard instructions to the jury: that they were to presume the defendant innocent unless or until the presentation of evidence was sufficient to dispel reasonable doubt. That opening statements were not to be taken as any such evidence, but merely as an outline of what each attorney hoped to demonstrate. And so on.

Kamin delivered his opening statement first, and he said what I expected. "Abel Nathanson cuts an impressive and sympathetic figure," he began. "For years, as New York City's only non-profit industrial developer, he snagged every grant, award and government subsidy in sight. Ladies and gentlemen of the jury, that means he used *your* hard-earned tax dollars to fund his ambitions. And beyond that, he cultivated the trust and the backing of countless elected officials, foundations and civic groups."

He went on this way for quite a while, painting Abel as a con artist, raking in praise and prestige and public funds while siphoning stolen tax dollars into his pocket.

Then I rose to make my own statement, present my own picture of Abel Nathanson, and of course mine was like a photographic negative of Kamin's, white in all the places his was black. Abel was a tireless crusader for all that was time-honored and true in our national commerce. He kept the American Dream alive for skilled laborers who would otherwise be forced to languish in the service sector. I went on for more than ten minutes about his many impressive accomplishments, his contributions to various charities, his adoption of an orphan, his triumph over his own disability. The dog was in the courtroom, stretched at Abel's feet, and if I could have had Lulu there as well, I would have.

Eventually I came around to the crime in question. "Like any successful man, Abel Nathanson has his rivals. And unfortunately for him, his would stop at nothing to bring him down. John Bonney, Mr. Nathanson's bitterest enemy, sent a decoy to meet with him during a time of dire financial stress for a member of his family. The mission was straightforward: to make Mr. Nathanson an offer he couldn't refuse—one in which the welfare of his sister was the bait. And the sole purpose of this offer, ladies and gentlemen, was to lure him into corporate fraud.

"The kind of deal this decoy proposed to Mr. Nathanson is offered—and accepted—every hour of every day in the construction industry," I went on. "Of course that doesn't make it right. But it does raise the question of why the district attorney is acting as if Abel Nathanson cracked Fort Knox. Ladies and gentlemen, I want you to ask yourselves what the D.A.—who hopes to occupy the mayor's office next year—has to gain from doing the bidding of John Bonney, who has underwritten so many political campaigns. And beyond that, I want you to ask yourselves one further question: what will it mean to *you*, to *us*, to the very American Dream I invoked a few moments ago, if our justice system can be bent to the will of the highest bidder?"

I let this question linger in the air for a moment before resuming my seat, and then Judge Jenner asked Kamin to call his first witness.

"The prosecution calls Nanette Magdalene to the stand," he said, and from the corner of my eye, I saw Abel clench his jaw.

Nan's appearance was perfect for strategic purposes. She wore one of her high-necked blouses and a knee-length skirt, and her hair was held back in a simple chignon. She looked slender and self-possessed and feminine and fragile. I watched the faces of the jurors as she was sworn in, and I could see she had their sympathy even before Kamin began.

"Please state your name."

"Nan Magdalene."

"Ms. Magdalene, in 2006 and 2007, what was your job?"

"I was Abel Nathanson's executive assistant."

A few details of her job description were established and then Kamin got down to business.

"Ms. Magdalene, did Tom Roscoe meet with Abel Nathanson in the latter's office on March twenty-seventh of last year?"

"He did."

"Would you please tell the court what they discussed that day?"

"I wasn't privy to much of the meeting," Nan began. "They were in the conference room, which isn't within earshot of the reception desk. But when Abel's next appointment arrived, I went to let him know. The conference room door was ajar and I caught just a fragment of their conversation."

"Do you have a clear memory of what was said?"

"Yes, I do."

"Please tell the court what you overheard."

"Well, Abel wanted a quote for work on his sister's house. I heard him ask what it would cost her for a roof replacement as well as a new septic tank and field."

"And then?"

"And then Mr. Roscoe said, 'Well, listen, not only will I give you a good deal on that side stuff, but I can hide the residential charges in the Navy Yard bill.' "

This surprised me. I'd expected Nan's version of the story to have the proposal coming from Abel.

Kamin was surprised too; ever so fleetingly, his face betrayed this. But after no more than the slightest pause, he spoke again.

"And how did Mr. Nathanson respond to that?"

Nan's voice was calm and clear. "He said, 'That's very tempting, but I'm afraid I can't consider it.' "

Kamin stood very still. Then slowly he tilted his head and

addressed his witness with great deliberation. "Ms. Magdalene. Your answer just now is in direct opposition to testimony you provided a short while ago. Would you please clarify what you just said?"

"Absolutely. Lest there be any confusion on this point: Abel Nathanson immediately refused Mr. Roscoe's offer."

A murmur rose in the courtroom. I shot a sidelong glance at Abel, but he looked just as stunned as I felt.

Kamin turned to the judge. "Your honor, I hereby move to declare Nan Magdalene a hostile witness."

I'd heard of this, but in my whole career, I'd never seen it happen. Once the judge consented, Kamin would resume his questions, but now he would be cross-examining her. He lost no time.

He approached the witness stand with a sheaf of papers. "Ms. Magdalene, here I have your sworn testimony from May eleventh of this year." He flipped to the final page. "Tell us please: is this your signature?"

"It is."

"Here you state that Abel Nathanson asked Mr. Roscoe whether he could discreetly transfer a private residential invoice to his non-profit's publicly funded bill for work done on the Brooklyn Navy Yard. Do you remember testifying to this version of what happened?"

"Of course I do."

"Then how do you account for telling the court a very different story today?"

"I was coerced into providing my false testimony of May eleventh."

"Coerced? In what way?" he asked. "And by whom?"

"By the man behind this whole scheme to frame Abel Nathanson. I was blackmailed by John Bonney."

In nearly a decade of watching him try cases, I had never seen Kamin so flustered. He was incredulous, stupefied. "By *John Bonney*?"

"It's exactly as Ms. Reeve has just said. John Bonney wanted to destroy my former boss. He paid a visit to my apartment one evening, before any of this began, and showed me compromising photographs he'd taken of me. He told me he would send them to the convent unless I helped him frame my employer."

"The convent?"

"I was raised by an order of Carmelite nuns. They're the only family I have in the world. And seeing such photographs would have devastated them beyond my power to describe. I can't begin to put into words how terrible it would have been."

Kamin recovered his composure. He turned to the judge. "Your honor, I have no further questions for the moment."

I understood. *Never ask a question unless you already know the answer.* Kamin realized he was in over his head, that there was no telling what this witness would unleash. And even though I could be no more certain than Kamin about what Nan would or wouldn't say, I was on my feet before my opponent had returned to the prosecution table.

"Ms. Magdalene, you mentioned compromising photographs of yourself in John Bonney's possession. What did you mean by 'compromising'?"

Nan's answer was straightforward. "John Bonney was a frequent customer at an establishment called the Nutcracker Suite, where visitors pay to engage in sadomasochistic activity. I was an employee there. Unbeknownst to me at the time, he took pictures of me while I was naked, bound and blindfolded. Unfortunately, even while wearing a blindfold, I can be identified beyond doubt by the burn scar on my left arm."

And here she unbuttoned the cuff of her blouse and pulled

the sleeve up to reveal an angry red splash between her wrist and elbow.

The murmur in the courtroom rose to a din. Judge Jenner banged her gavel and called for silence.

"And Ms. Magdalene, you've testified here that with these photographs, John Bonney blackmailed you into framing Mr. Nathanson. Could you please tell the court what you meant by that?"

"The only hard evidence that Mr. Nathanson allegedly engaged in fraud," she said, "are two estimates, bearing his signature, that were signed within 48 hours of each other. They are a list of exactly the same line items, but on the second one, the charges have been inflated in several instances, resulting in a forty thousand dollar difference. The fact that he signed the second so soon after the first—endorsing tens of thousands of dollars in additional costs for exactly the same job— would naturally warrant suspicion that something was amiss."

"Yes, it would," I said carefully. I was well acquainted with these two documents. "Can you provide an explanation for Mr. Nathanson's signature on the second set of estimates?"

"I can," she said. "As was our practice, on the afternoon that he signed the second set, I put the pen in his hand. I told Abel he was signing a document associated with a grant proposal. And then I set his hand on the line."

Again, a hum of consternation from the gallery; again, a call to order.

"And this deception was what John Bonney required of you in exchange for keeping the aforementioned photographs to himself?"

"Yes, this deception and my testimony of May eleventh."

I felt light-headed with astonishment. "I have no further questions."

Kamin had risen again and now he advanced on Nan with renewed determination.

"If this alleged threat of blackmail held such potential *devastation* for you," he asked her, outright mockery in his tone, "then how have you found the sudden resolve to reveal those secrets here today—with no apparent shame or hesitation—before the court, the public and the press?"

"I said I would be devastated if the nuns were to learn of them," she said. "I don't care about other people knowing."

"Well—presuming what you've said has any basis in truth—wouldn't Mr. Bonney be as free to mail those pictures today as he was on the day of your deposition?"

"Yes, but he won't."

"What would stop him now?"

"I was so frightened and distraught when he first came to me," Nan said, "that I couldn't think clearly. But since then, it's occurred to me—regrettably late in the proceedings—that there was a way to ensure his discretion. On the specifics of that, I'll need to take the Fifth."

And for a moment there was not a sound in the courtroom. It was as if a collective breath had been caught and held. You could hear the slight din in the corridor just beyond the closed doors. Everyone in the room was momentarily stunned into silence: the judge, the attorneys, the jury, the spectators, even the defendant.

The proceedings after that are a blur in my memory. Kamin asked for a sidebar conference in the judge's chambers. There he requested a recess on grounds of surprise. And the next morning, he filed a motion to dismiss the case against Abel.

Technically speaking, it might have been the most unequivocal success of my legal career. But I left the courthouse all but unnoticed. The reporters and cameramen were like a feral pack of dogs, hot-eyed and hell-bent on just one person: Nan.

She was happy to talk to them, as it turned out. And happy to provide them with a photograph of her own, of a shirtless John Bonney at the end of a domme's flogger. It was on the cover of the *New York Post* the next morning, beneath the headline WHIPPING BOY BONNEY'S FOILED FRAME-UP.

12

"You know," I told Nan now, "most defense lawyers have a savior complex. But as good as the outcome was for Abel—and no client of mine has ever had a better one—I didn't save him. You did. Can't you go back to him at this point? Surely he would take you back now."

"No," she said. "It's not possible. It would never be the same as it was before. Too much has happened."

"Does that make you…sad?"

"Yes."

The waitress came over with the check and I handed her a credit card without looking at it.

"And the Lighthouse job?" I asked, when she'd moved away again. "How is that?"

"It's fine," she said. "Which is the most anything else could ever be."

"Please forgive this question," I said, "but I have to ask: why Abel? I mean, there's a great deal to admire about the man, but I don't understand the depth of feeling you've invested in him. What is that about?"

"I don't know," she said.

The waitress came back with the credit card slip and I picked up the pen she'd provided. I had asked Nan almost everything. The only questions left in my mind were logistical ones.

"How did you get that photograph of Bonney?" I asked, even though—having been to the Nutcracker—I could hazard a guess, and Nan confirmed it.

"They have hidden security cameras in each room. For a lot

of reasons. So the house would have some recourse if a client hurt one of the women. So there would be a record of what took place in a session if a client ever accused one of the dommes of seriously hurting him. Mistress DeVille kept a meticulous archive of these tapes going back two years."

"And you had access to this archive?"

"I'd worked there a long time," Nan said. "She trusted me."

"So you made stills from the videos," I guessed.

"Yes," she said, and smiled. "It's much easier to sell individual photographs to the media than it is to leak a tape. I sent them to Bonney's office by messenger the morning of the trial. I let him know I had the originals and that if he didn't persuade Kamin to drop the case within twenty-four hours, I would sell them to the press."

"And then, once the trial was over, you sold them anyway."

"Yes," she said, without a hint of apology in her tone. "The pictures supported the story I told on the stand. Without them, the public might think I was lying about everything."

A new question came to me now.

"If you had those photographs of Bonney," I said slowly. "If you had them all along—then why wait? If you'd threatened him earlier, he might have pulled some strings to avert the trial before it began."

"I didn't see Bonney's picture in the paper until the charges against Abel made the news," Nan said. "By then, Abel's reputation had been ruined. To me, it wasn't enough to keep him out of prison. I had to clear his name." She looked steadily across the table at me. "Maybe now he can even have the waterfront at Red Hook."

"You did clear his name," I said, "but at the expense of your own."

"Abel's the only person I really care about," she told me. "He knew about my past already. Who else would I worry about?"

"Well, just as you said in court. The nuns. The only family you've ever known."

"But again, they're a reclusive order. They don't read newspapers, they don't watch television. They don't talk to outsiders. How in the world would a tabloid story reach them?"

"Not the story. The photographs. You wouldn't answer this question in court, but since you're assured of confidentiality now: what's to stop John Bonney at this point from sending the photographs of you to the convent? If only for revenge?"

She stared at me for a long moment, as if unwilling to believe I could be so slow-witted. When she spoke again, her voice was gentle and almost pitying.

"There are no photographs of me. There never were."

"Bonney has no photos of you?"

"Of course not."

"Then how could he blackmail you?"

"Bonney never blackmailed me. He never even recognized me. He's a submissive himself, you understand. So when he came to the Nutcracker, I was never the one he wanted to see."

I sat back against the black vinyl, suddenly feeling the need for another drink, and a stronger one than beer.

"So," I said slowly. "The only one guilty of blackmail is you. And by dint of that, you've managed to take down an innocent man."

"Bonney is hardly an innocent man. He tried to destroy Abel. He masterminded the entrapment."

"But Abel walked into that trap of his own accord. He was hardly innocent either."

"Do you have any innocent clients, counselor?"

I didn't answer this.

"I'm not interested in innocence," she said after a moment.

"We're all fallen creatures. Clearly, neither man is an angel. But Abel's the devil I know." She smiled ever so slightly. "Or at least, the one I serve."

"From afar," I said. It wasn't a nice thing to say. Something about this woman—perhaps her indifference to anyone but Abel—remained an affront to me.

But she didn't seem put off by the remark. "From afar," she agreed. "That part has been difficult, I admit. But that's my fault, and my cross to bear." She tilted her head and added, "I learned that from the nuns."

Her undoing, as she'd long known, was in seeking affirmation of what should have remained ephemeral. Abel was right to dismiss her. Faith that couldn't endure without reassurance was no faith at all. Whenever she felt he should have let her stay, she remembered his warning of long ago. *There are some mistakes,* he had said, *that you can't make.*

He'd called her after the trial to thank her for saving him. That was the way he put it: saving him. Their conversation wasn't long—there was too much that neither of them would ever be able to say—but his voice was hoarse with gratitude. The memory of this made her exile endurable, though it still wasn't easy, and would never be easy.

Sometimes she thought the hardest cross, the hardest loss, to bear was not the privilege of assisting Abel, nor the steady and cherished routine, nor even the chance to pass her days in his presence, but the certainty of her understanding with him and the serenity it yielded. The way it tampered with the air and the sunlight even when she wasn't near him. Her sense of purpose and peace, her feeling of having a place in the world. And the way it carried her to and from the office, informing every sight she took in along her path.

Like the sparkle of broken glass pressed into the pavement. The trees along the sidewalk, flowering somehow from rain-starved roots. Lone gulls too far inland, adrift overhead. The open grates at the edges of the tire-scarred streets, where smoke was always rising from underground.

EPILOGUE

"What is this?" Stas asked, upon coming home to find the makings of a party on the side porch. It was an unseasonably warm night in February. Since screening in the porch and buying a heat lamp the autumn before, we liked to have dinner outside when it wasn't too cold. On the picnic table was a bottle of champagne, a tin of caviar and a little bakery cake.

Clara, who had been stacking blocks in the corner, came running to Stas. Four-month-old Leo slept in the plastic swing that hung from the rafters.

"I knew you were in meetings all day and I didn't want to tell you this by voicemail," I told him. "But Lily had her baby this morning!"

"Ah! Well, this is very fine news," he said, picking up Clara and hugging her. "But I thought she was not due for another two weeks."

"She wasn't. The baby came early."

"Is it a boy or a girl?"

"A boy. He's almost eight pounds and his name is Hilton William."

"Hilton?" Stas said, taking a seat at the table and reaching for the champagne. "Like the hotel?"

"Yes, exactly. I asked the same thing. Apparently Lily's sure he was conceived in a Hilton hotel room. She said it was a very special night."

"I see. Very well, then. Though I am glad this special night did not happen in a Super 8."

This made me laugh. But then I'd been laughing with joy all

day. The birth was still a miracle to me. Lily and Darren had been trying to have a baby for so long. I'd even come to believe they'd made their peace with the way things were. But these past nine months, she and Darren were unmistakably so much happier that I wondered how I'd ever thought they were happy before. And while I knew this was because of Lily's pregnancy, I couldn't help thinking it was also about whatever had happened in that hotel room.

"In other news," I said now, nodding at the moving van parked outside the house next door, "I think we've finally got neighbors."

"Do they look nice?"

"I haven't actually seen them. I've only seen the moving guys. But I guess we'll know soon enough."

Months had gone by before a new company took over the construction of that house, and it was several more months before it was finished. I wondered whether the buyers knew that a man had been killed inside it and buried beneath it.

After struggling for more than a minute with the bottle of champagne, unable to peel away the seal around the cork, Stas reached for his boot knife and cut it away.

I'd seen my husband draw his knife a dozen times before. And yet just for an instant, within this festive setting, it was a jarring sight: the glint of a blade slipped from a boot. Or maybe I was just unsettled by the mention of the house next door.

"Did I ever tell you," I asked abruptly, "that for a while there, I thought you'd killed Jack?"

Stas raised an eyebrow. "No, you never did," he said. "Is this true?"

"Yes."

"When was this?"

"When the detective told us he was likely dead." I smiled at him now, and made my tone light, as if I were joking. "I sus-pected you right away."

"I see," he said after a long moment. He twisted the top of the champagne bottle and there was the violent sound of a pop-ping cork. "And how did you feel about being married to a murderer?"

I wasn't sure whether he was nettled or amused.

"Well," I said. What could I say? I would never tell him how frightened I'd felt, how disoriented and distressed and alone. I would never tell anyone, let alone Stas, how my anguish gave way to arousal, or how dismayed I was to learn he was innocent. "I didn't know how to feel, really."

"Were you afraid of me?"

"Not really. Maybe a little."

"Too bad that didn't last," my husband said, and his tone was as light as mine had been a moment ago.

The sun dropped behind the pines in the vacant lot across the street and a wind rustled the trees. Sitting there, listening to the locusts seething beyond the screen, I had a sudden dizzying sense of how scant a shelter we had here, how precar-ious it all was: the few planks underfoot that kept us above the dirt, the lanterns that we lit against the gathering dusk.

Then Stas folded his knife and replaced it in his boot. He poured two flutes of champagne, nudged one of them toward me and lifted the other.

"To family," he said. And we drank.

JOYLAND

by STEPHEN KING

College student Devin Jones took the summer job at Joyland hoping to forget the girl who broke his heart. But he wound up facing something far more terrible: the legacy of a vicious murder, the fate of a dying child, and dark truths about life— and what comes after—that would change his world forever.

A riveting story about love and loss, about growing up and growing old—and about those who don't get to do either because death comes for them before their time—JOYLAND is Stephen King at the peak of his storytelling powers. With all the emotional impact of King masterpieces such as *The Green Mile* and *The Shawshank Redemption*, JOYLAND is at once a mystery, a horror story, and a bittersweet coming-of-age novel, one that will leave even the most hard-boiled reader profoundly moved.

ACCLAIM FOR STEPHEN KING:

"An immensely talented storyteller of seemingly inexhaustible gifts."
— Interview

"Stephen King is so widely acknowledged as America's master of paranormal terrors that you can forget his real genius is for the everyday."
— New York Times

"Stephen King is superb."
— Time